AF605003

# ENGLISH MYTHS

# ENGLISH MYTHS

## FROM KING ARTHUR AND THE HOLY GRAIL TO GEORGE AND THE DRAGON

MICHAEL KERRIGAN

amber
BOOKS

First published in 2022



Published by
Amber Books Ltd
United House
North Road
London
N7 9DP
United Kingdom
www.amberbooks.co.uk
Instagram: amberbooksltd
Facebook: amberbooks
Twitter: @amberbooks

ISBN: 978-1-83886-171-1

Project Editor: Michael Spilling
Designer: Mark Batley
Picture Research: Terry Forshaw

Printed in China

# CONTENTS

# INTRODUCTION

England's very history is mythic. At least, it started out in mystery and legend. Only slowly did something like a factual narrative emerge.

OPPOSITE: **Brutus does battle with the giants in this medieval illustration from Geoffrey of Monmouth's *History*. The giants' defeat opened the way to the building of cities, in this case London.**

The seamen's cries cut the quiet of the cold grey dawn; the rhythmic murmur of the waves was interrupted by the grating of the wooden keel against the gravel of the beach. Their rest disturbed, white gulls rose like wraiths and fell like snowflakes, mewling indignantly as they circled on the morning breeze.

As the ship jarred and shuddered to an awkward halt and sailors leapt ashore and splashed through the shallows to secure it, their commander stood there silently transfixed. As they made to help their mates aboard the vessels running up beside them, he didn't just ignore them; he all but disappeared. Withdrawing into the folds of the great cloak he'd wrapped around his shoulders, he stood there rigid, his posture frozen, his face gaunt and harrowed, staring in something like alarm at the landscape that awaited

ABOVE: **Brutus the Trojan sets sail for Britain, from *The History of the Kings of Britain* by Geoffrey of Monmouth, from a fifteenth century manuscript.**

them. Its features were still hard to discern in the drear half-light of early morning, but its menace was unmistakeable even so. Silhouetted trees crowded down to the high-water mark; clothed the slopes above all the way to the skyline: no sign of human habitation was to be seen.

## Taking flight

Just a few days before, Prince Brutus of Troy had set out from the coast of Gaul, his closest comrades sailing with him in this little flotilla. There was nothing here to compare with the carefully tended fields and neat villages he'd left behind. Still less did this wild country resemble the city of Alba Longa in Latium, where he'd been born. Brutus was the son of Ascanius, himself the child of the Trojan hero Aeneas – whose wife Creusa had been the daughter of King Priam. Ultimately, indeed, they had both been divinely descended – Aeneas from Aphrodite, goddess of love, and Creusa from Jupiter, god of the heavens – but these glittering antecedents hadn't helped them when it mattered most.

At the end of a 10-year siege, their country's Greek invaders had finally found their way through Troy's formidable defences. They had tricked their way in, inside their notorious 'gift' of a giant wooden horse. Emerging stealthily through a trapdoor in its belly after night had fallen, they had murdered the city's sentries and thrown its gates wide open so their waiting comrades could surge in, taking the sleeping citizenry by surprise.

A spree of slaughter and destruction had followed and, as Troy's topless towers came crashing down in flames around them, Aeneas and his dependents had been forced into flight. Aeneas had led the way, carrying his aged father Anchises on his shoulders; young Ascanius had stumbled along with Creusa in the rear. They had made it to the safety of a ship and put to sea. Ahead of them lay long years of wandering, years of fighting, first in Sicily, and then in central Italy, where every local tribe had been arrayed against them. Ultimately, though, they had won and, generations later, descendants of theirs founded the city that would go on ultimately to win renown as Rome.

Brutus would be but a distant memory by that time, though. Right now his situation was anything but glorious. He had, the story goes, accidentally killed his father with an arrow: he'd been banished from Italy, forced to make his own way through the world. In its way, though, his destiny was not to be too unlike that of his father and his grandfather: endless war and seemingly endless wandering. Landing in France, he'd fought the native tribes to found the city of Turones – Tours, in the Loire Valley. Before too long, though, he'd had to move on once more.

## An unpromising start

Another dawn, another country; new enemies to be overcome and territories to be tamed ... Now Brutus had it all to do again. The good news was that this island at the very end of the world turned out to have no human inhabitants to be subdued; the bad news was, that it was home to monstrous giants. Brutus and his companions had made their landing on the southern coast of Devon, not far from Totnes, the story goes.

The giants weren't in a welcoming mood. Under the leadership of the grotesque Goemagot, or Gogmagog, they descended on the interlopers with mayhem on their minds. But Brutus and his warriors were not cowed. They fought back ferociously – they knew their lives depended on their courage and resolve – and finally they started to prevail.

**THE GIANTS WEREN'T IN A WELCOMING MOOD. UNDER THE LEADERSHIP OF THE GROTESQUE GOEMAGOT, OR GOGMAGOG, THEY DESCENDED ON THE INTERLOPERS WITH MAYHEM ON THEIR MINDS.**

Eventually, all the giants had been killed apart from Goemagot himself. He challenged Brutus to nominate a champion to wrestle him to the death. Corineus was the appointed hero: after an excruciatingly long and increasingly frantic struggle, he threw Goemagot off a cliff to his death at the place that is nowadays known as Salcombe. (The episode is commemorated in the name 'Salcombe' itself, derived from the Latin *Saltus Goemagot*

– 'Goemagot's Leap'.) The sea below was stained by the giant's blood. As was the section of the coast that it lapped up against. To this day you can see, tucked away behind the ruins of Salcombe's sixteenth-century castle, an area low down where the rocks are a striking red. Corineus, meanwhile, is memorialized in the name of the county of Cornwall. And, of course, the country as a whole was to become known as 'Britain', Brutus's name being gradually corrupted over centuries.

## Tall stories

No modern scholar seriously believes any of the above. The tale of Troy, its siege and fall, belongs to classic legend. As do the subsequent adventures of Aeneas. We owe what we 'know' of Brutus's story to the anonymous ninth-century *Historia Brittonum* ('History of the Britons'), whose account was filled out by Geoffrey of Monmouth (c. 1095–1155), in his *Historia Regum Britaniae* ('History of the Kings of Britain'). Even his own contemporaries confessed themselves sceptical of Geoffrey's account, much as they might have liked to believe it.

**BELOW: So scant was the mythic record on England's foundation that the single giant Goemagot was often afterwards assumed to have been two individuals, 'Gog' and 'Magog'.**

MAGOG

GOG

## Poetry and prestige

ABOVE: **Geoffrey of Monmouth isn't a historian at all by modern standards, but as a mytho-historical chronicler he is beyond compare.**

No sooner do we debunk such stories, though, than we start to see their real worth. In the first place, there is their sheer entertainment value. Who seriously wants to be told about narrow, steeply sloping valleys when they might be hearing about brave heroes slaying giants? So much more appealing can myths come to be over the dreary record of reality that they take on a special transcendent status. They may not actually be 'true' in the most mundanely literal sense but it feels as though they 'should' be; it seems appropriate to the prestige of a people or a state.

Myth brings poetry to a history that can be all too prosaic. When its tales are told eloquently enough, they can be sublime. Not only had the Fall of Troy been epically recorded in the *Iliad* of Homer (a blind poet of the eighth century BCE whose existence may well itself have been entirely mythic); the adventures of Aeneas and his family in its aftermath had famously been recorded by the Roman poet Virgil (70–19 BCE), in his *Aeneid.* This elaborately wrought unabashedly literary epic had furnished the vast and powerful empire of Augustus with an origin myth that its earliest readers could see as being commensurate with the greatness of their state.

Most civilizations in history have had such myths in some shape or form. The story of Brutus's wanderings, his arrival on the Devon coast and his war with the giants gives England an origin myth that is all its own. But it can also be seen to do a great deal more. By furnishing a narrative link between the histories of England and classical Greece and Rome, it places a chilly and rainswept country (with as yet no claim on greatness or glory) on a par with those celebrated civilizations of antiquity. So it isn't too difficult to see why readers in the England of the Middle Ages would have badly wanted to believe the Brutus story.

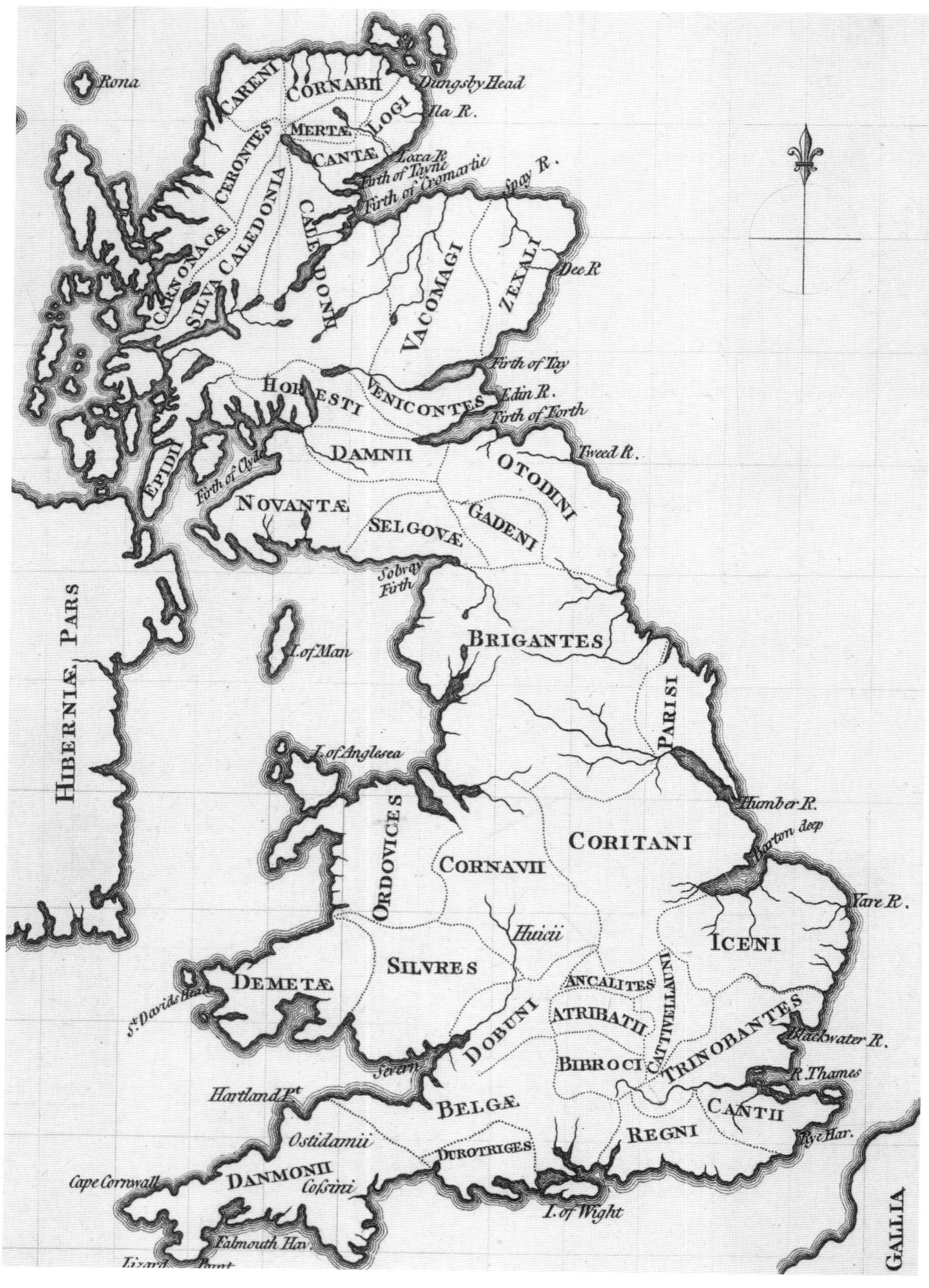
Rona
CARENI
CORNABII
Dungsby Head
Ila R.
MERTÆ
LOGI
CERONTES
CANTÆ
Loxa R.
Firth of Tayne
Firth of Cromartie
Spay R.
CALEDONII
SILVA CALEDONIA
CARNONACÆ
VACOMAGI
ZEXALI
Dee R.
Firth of Tay
HORESTI
VENICONTES
Edin R.
Firth of Forth
DAMNII
Tweed R.
OTODINI
EPIDII
Firth of Clyde
NOVANTÆ
SELGOVÆ
GADENI
Solway Firth
HIBERNIÆ PARS
I. of Man
BRIGANTES
PARISI
I. of Anglesea
Humber R.
ORDOVICES
CORITANI
Barton deep
CORNAVII
Yare R.
Huicii
ICENI
SILVRES
DEMETÆ
ANCALITES
St. Davids Head
ATRIBATII
CATTIVELLAUNI
TRINOBANTES
DOBUNI
Blackwater R.
BIBROCI
Severn
R. Thames
Hartland Pt.
BELGÆ
CANTII
Ostidamii
REGNI
Rye Har.
DUROTRIGES
Cape Cornwall
DANMONII
Cosiriri
I. of Wight
Falmouth Hav.
GALLIA

## Myth and countermyth

Not that it has necessarily been eager to acknowledge this. When Shakespeare's John of Gaunt (in Richard II, c. 1595) spoke of his homeland as a 'sceptred isle', a 'throne of kings', he laid emphasis on the way he saw Nature as having equipped his country as a 'fortress'. The 'silver sea' around, he said, formed a protective 'moat', just like a castle's. The imagery is vivid, and on the face of it convincing: 40-odd kilometres (26-plus miles) of open, sometimes stormy, water is an obstacle indeed.

Historically, however, the sea has been as much an open roadway as a barrier – especially in times when progress overland was so much slower and more arduous than it is now. In medieval times, the traveller tended to see the open water as an invitation: wayfaring ashore – over mountains, across bleak moorlands and through thick forests and treacherous swamps – was the real challenge. So it certainly was in the early centuries of England's history: a succession of invading and occupying forces came across the sea, each one changing the country and helping to shape its future.

**OPPOSITE: The efforts of the early-modern 'antiquarians' seem more like mythology now than history. This eighteenth century antiquarian map purports to show the territories of Britain's Celtic 'tribes' before the Romans came.**

## Pedestrian passage

Like their successors, the first Englishmen and -women were also incomers from continental Europe. Unlike them, however, they do appear to have made the journey overland.

During the great glaciations, which started around two and a half million years ago and didn't end till about 10,000 years ago, so much water could be locked up in ice sheets anything up to 3.2km (2 miles) deep that sea levels were much lower than today. At times 125m (410ft) lower, which for lengthy periods (hundreds of millennia at a time) left what is now the English Channel and southern sections of the North Sea completely high and dry, though boggy in places and scored across by streams. (England's Thames and France's Seine formed a single river.)

'Doggerland', as this dry area was called (there's a broad 'Dogger Bank' beneath the North Sea to this day), might not unreasonably be described as a land bridge, though that would perhaps imply that conscious crossings were being made. These communities probably weren't aware of journeying at all. Their

**RIGHT: The Swanscombe Skull was one of several fossil fragments found at the West Sussex site in 1935–6. Representing *Homo heidelbergensis*, it is believed to have belonged to a young woman.**

hunter-gatherer lifestyle was nomadic by nature. Although they were always on the move – following migrating herds; seeking out the best sources of berries, nuts or shellfish – they weren't really 'travelling' as we would understand it.

## Tabula rasa

The earliest signs (stone tools and footprints) of such peoples to be found in England were left by a hominid ancestor of modern humans some 900,000 years ago on what is now the Norfolk coast. The oldest actual fossil remains that excavations have uncovered date from more like half a million years ago. Traces of Homo heidelbergensis were found by researchers in West Sussex, and Neanderthal remains turned up in Kent.

We don't know what became of any of these communities. The earliest evidence of modern humans (Homo sapiens) living in England dates back only 40,000 years, and the country doesn't seem to have been continuously occupied until about 10,000 BCE, by which time Europe was entering what the experts call the Neolithic or the New Stone Age. The great innovation that gave this period its name was the introduction of agriculture and the settling down of people into static, fixed communities that this brought with it.

Nomadic hunter-gatherers have to travel light; it's no surprise that they should have left no great archaeological legacy beyond the odd arrowhead or stone blade. Farmers have huts and villages, though; they mark the ground when they work it with their ditches and embankments – even the furrows they make can sometimes endure. Over time, indeed, discrepancies of power and rank emerge, and the accumulation of wealth and treasure begins. The prestige of individuals or of entire communities begins to be asserted in impressive works in earth and stone.

## Say it with stones

We get tantalizing hints of the ritual and spiritual life of the people of Neolithic England from the more enduring monuments they left behind. At a cluster of sites in Wiltshire, for example. The earthen 'barrow' or burial mound at West Kennet was built some time around 3650 BCE and the bodies of up to 50 people were placed inside in cavernous chambers constructed out of great slabs of stone. Not far away, at Avebury, a remarkable henge – a complex of earthworks and stone circles – was constructed from around 3000 BCE. It's very different in its appearance from Stonehenge – begun about the same time and not too far away – but we've no real way of accounting for this difference.

**THE SEA BELOW WAS STAINED BY THE GIANT'S BLOOD.**

Any more than we have of explaining the purpose of the carefully built and beautifully symmetrical chalk mound raised up at Silbury Hill from around 2400 BCE. At the very least, though, such sites bring home to us the fact that the people of the Neolithic had a religious and ritualistic dimension to their lives. And consequently, it seems fair to say, an imaginative and a mythic one.

## Mythic might-have-beens

Even so, it has to be acknowledged that we really know very little about life as it was lived in England in these earliest prehistoric times. And still less about the stories people told. We can guess, on the basis of what has been learned of the mythologies of other hunter-gatherer communities around the world that have survived into modern times and been studied by anthropologists, that they had their own narratives explaining how their universe

Its origins as misty as the Wiltshire dawn, the henge at Avebury extends over 28 acres. We can only guess at its spiritual or ceremonial function now.

came to be and how it was organized. It's likely too that they told tales about important 'totem' animals they hunted.

To myths like these, the Neolithic would have needed to add stories to account for the fertility of the earth, the impact of the weather and the cycle of the seasons. Most crucially, for the 'death' of the sun in winter and its return in spring. The earliest English farmers must have felt an all but vertiginous sense of helplessness as the winter solstice approached in the cold and dark each year. Through much of the modern world, winter may be at its worst an annual inconvenience; for many millennia, though, it brought societies to the brink.

Where records do exist of ancient mythologies – as they do for the early civilizations of Mesopotamia or Egypt, say – they generally address these natural phenomena along with eternal human concerns such as love and war. It was probably the same in Neolithic Europe. But we know absolutely nothing of any specifics. Prehistoric England won't have been a blank slate culturally, we can be certain, but it isn't one we can even begin to read.

**BELOW: Rising abruptly out of the Wiltshire countryside, Silbury Hill stands 39.3m (129ft) high.**

## Celtic confusion

Things don't get much clearer until the advent of the Celts, in around 500 BCE. However, given that they appear to have had a

religious taboo against written script, we can't 'read' their culture in any more literal sense either.

Among the many mysteries surrounding the Celts is where they came from originally. In the historical record, for as long as there has been one, they have been associated with the western fringe of Europe – a loose line of countries stretching down from Scotland through Ireland, Wales and Cornwall to Brittany and then to Galicia, in northwestern Spain.

That isn't necessarily where they originated, though. It's evident that, for much of the mid-first millennium BCE, the Celts were established across almost all of western, central and southern Europe – and even into the edge of Asia, in what is now Turkey. Whatever their ultimate origins, their long-term relegation to Europe's western margins only came later, when they were pushed out of prime territories by an expanding Roman Empire. Predominantly mountainous, wet and marshy, these areas abutting the Atlantic would be afflicted by poverty and famine well into recent times. The Romans were content to leave them unconquered, or at least only sparsely settled.

**FOR MUCH OF THE MID-FIRST MILLENNIUM BCE, THE CELTS WERE ESTABLISHED ACROSS ALMOST ALL OF WESTERN, CENTRAL AND SOUTHERN EUROPE – AND EVEN INTO THE EDGE OF ASIA.**

For a long time, experts argued (and some still do) that these Atlantic-dwellers started out from central Europe and pushed out from there to the four points of the compass. More recently, researchers have pointed to signs that the Celts were indeed originally settled along western Europe's Atlantic seaboard and that they expanded from there across the continent as a whole.

## Invasion? Migration? Diffusion?

That said, the mystery of the Celts for us lies at least in part in the limitations of our modern understanding of what a people is, and what their appearance in a place might mean. Although it isn't incorrect to talk of the 'coming of the Celts' to England, we do have to be careful that we understand what that probably entailed. The same might be said of the idea that they arrived in England as 'invaders', or even that their movement represented a 'migration'.

The great expansion of the Celts appears actually to have been an ad hoc series of forays by little warbands led by adventurer-chieftains. We know that such events took place:

**ABOVE: Framed by the ruins of a sixteenth-century church, the Celtic cross at St Dwynwen's, Anglesey, is a reminder of the role the Celts would ultimately play in Christianizing Britain as a whole.**

they've been described in detail by Greek and Roman writers. In around 391 BCE, for instance, a Celtic army sacked Rome. Just over a century later (279 BCE) another force destroyed the sacred shrine of Delphi, Greece, and killed the priestess there.

The idea of the Celtic warrior was by no means mythic, then, but it does unjustly overshadow other, less exciting but maybe more important, forms of contact. Some researchers believe that much of the Celts' contact with the wider ancient world took place through the medium of commerce. Trade was as important as warfare, they say: expeditions were undertaken by intrepid merchants, ready to exchange luxury craft-goods for food and wine. We know from the weaponry they left behind, and the accounts the classical writers gave of them, that the Celts pursued a warrior ideal. We don't know how far down the social scale this aspiration extended or for how many fighting would really have been a normal way of life.

## Cultural domination

Either way, the Celts ventured far and wide across continental Europe – and the British Isles – taking tribute, or commercial profits, from communities on the ground. Whether they were actually invaders or not, they were certainly cultural conquerors.

Everything from their ornate art and weaponry to their religious beliefs were taken up across their range. Their priests, or druids, held their ceremonies in sacred groves of oak trees. Their rituals centred on human sacrifice, the classical observers said. This could have been a smear, but wasn't necessarily. Archaeological evidence suggests that it might well be true.

The Celts don't seem to have established any larger, more coherent overarching empire, though, even if there's ample evidence that they established themselves as local chieftains across their territories. (Or at least that local chieftains were enthusiastic adopters of the Celtic lifestyle. Again, it's hard to know quite how literally the Celts 'conquered' where their way prevailed.)

Nor can we be sure how deeply the peoples who were 'Celticized' were actually changed. A certain amount of interbreeding will undoubtedly have taken place. In the absence of any wholesale population movement, though, it's an oversimplification to see these 'Celts' – the peoples of what we now regard as the 'Celtic countries' – as genuinely representing a distinct 'race'. So although it may be more or less accepted in

BELOW: **The most famous Celtic 'bard', Ossian was himself, appropriately, more or less mythical. His 'works' were cooked up by the Scottish poet James Macpherson (1736–96).**

ABOVE & RIGHT: **Celtic Iron Age torques, such as the first century BCE Great Torque of Snettisham (above), banished the idea that Celtic craftwork was crude or in any way 'barbaric'.**

modern parlance to speak of the Welsh or Irish, say, as Celtic nations, it is really only very loosely true.

## From monuments to monks

Like the peoples of the Neolithic era, the Celts left a monumental record. Hill forts like those at Old Oswestry in Shropshire (c. 1000 BCE) or Maiden Castle, Dorset, (c. 800 BCE) may have been functional, but the White Horse at Uffington, Oxfordshire, believed to have been carved out in the latter part of the first millennium BCE, surely represents a more religious, or at least more imaginative, dimension of Celtic creativity. We've no way of knowing what story it tells, though, or what it means.

The Celts clearly did have a mythology – and an extremely rich and complex one. For many generations, though, this was not written down. We know it existed because the stories were passed around by word of mouth, and survived by re-telling down the generations until well into the Christian era when Irish monks recorded them in their manuscripts.

And reinterpreted them. As clergymen, they could hardly be expected to sign up to an old pagan pantheon. They recast what had been gods and goddesses in the old tales they were translating from Irish into medieval Latin as heroes or heroines and giants. Or as *aes sidhe* – the Irish fairy folk. They dwelt in a separate but adjacent dimension to mortal men and women, but strayed back and forth across the boundary between the two. (Sometimes, indeed, they abducted infants or even adult men or women and kept them with them in their own realm for a time.) More than mortal humans, but less than deities, all these different

### Bad Press

Their refusal to embrace literacy left the Celts in the unenviable position of being written up by their enemies, whose accounts are the only 'history' they have. They were always barbarians as far as classical authors were concerned.

Sometimes their freedom from civilization and its corrupting effects was held up for praise – a stick with which to beat a 'soft' and 'decadent' Greek or Roman culture. Mostly, though, it was seen as savagery. That they dressed their hair with white clay and painted their faces to do battle would have set them down as all but bestial to the Greeks and Romans even if they hadn't collected the heads of their conquered enemies.

Actually, they did a great many other things, too, many of them demanding the highest technological understanding, skill and artistry: everything from building roads to creating stunning jewellery.

**ABOVE: Julius Caesar lands in the face of fierce resistance from local tribesmen in the first, ill-fated Roman invasion of England, which took place in 55 BCE. Aulus Plautius would fare better almost a century later.**

kinds of characters kept the Celtic mythic tradition alive without upsetting the new Christian accord.

## *Veni, vidi, vici*

By the end of the first millennium BCE, England was as Celtic as Connemara or the Hebrides. But the arrival of the Romans changed all that. They definitely did come as invaders – though, even then, their conquest was so slow and faltering that it could feel more like an endless process than a sudden fait accompli.

*Veni, vidi, vici* ('I came, I saw, I conquered'), boasted Julius Caesar (100–44 BCE) notoriously. The reality doesn't seem to have been anything like so brisk. He certainly came, in 55 BCE, but what he saw was very much a Celtic country – of which he wasn't to conquer more than a few square kilometres. Local tribesmen quickly sent him packing; and though he came back the following year with a bigger and stronger force, he fared only marginally better this second time.

Not until nearly a century later, in 43 CE, was a successful invasion mounted by a Roman force under Aulus Plautius, who conquered that part of England that lay south of the River Humber and east of the Trent. The southeast, in other words – to this day the country's richest corner. Successive generals took further territories, until under Gnaeus Julius Agricola (40–93 CE), the whole of England, much of Wales and a slice of Scotland constituted the Roman province of Britannia.

Along with this went the wholesale Romanization of the local, Celtic culture. The Romans were great centralizers, who stamped their own civilizational template on the territories they took. They had an all but religious belief in the value of regimentation, in everything from rhetoric to roadbuilding, from art and literature to schools and city planning. In their actual religious thinking they could be unexpectedly open, though.

They'd shown this quality from early on. As Italic tribespeople in their pre-Roman times they'd followed an anarchy of local earth-cults. Once they'd established themselves as a regional power, however, with self-consciously civilized aspirations, they'd taken a ready-made pantheon of gods and goddesses from the Greeks. Zeus, god of the heavens, wielder of lightning bolts, had become Jupiter; his Olympus-dwelling wife Hera had become the Roman Juno; love-goddess Aphrodite had become Venus, and so on.

As might be expected, they imposed this religion (with all its accompanying myths) wherever they went. Temples were built to honour these deities across the Roman world.

## THE ROAD NOT TAKEN

With the rise of the Roman Empire, Celtic culture was marginalized, both geographically and in prestige, becoming an object of condescension if not contempt. Almost as quickly, though, came a backlash: by the end of the first century, the Roman historian Tacitus (c. 56–c. 120 BCE), was expressing admiration for the Celts' indomitable fighting spirit; their refusal to bow the knee to Roman rule.

This romanticization was to continue, the appeal of the Celtic countries lying precisely in their ungovernable wildness – their outsider status in relation to the European mainstream. From this perspective, the Celtic countries acquired vaguely exotic associations as realms of mystery and magic, of bardic lyricism and epic poetry.

Some sort of Celtic memory would endure in the Arthurian romances of the high-medieval period. Their rediscovery after the Industrial Revolution brought an all-important touch of enchantment to English myth for readers in rebellion against the rampant materialism of their age. Tantalizingly, too, it seemed to suggest an alternative course England's history might have taken – a more colourful and creative one, maybe.

## Local exceptions

They did, however, show some flexibility in certain circumstances. Especially in territories that were as far from the imperial centre as Britannia was. And above all in the early days of occupation, significant compromises seem to have been made. In some cases, a degree of authority was delegated to Celtic 'client' kings. The Romans certainly allowed the worship of their gods to become associated with previously existing local cults.

Hence what happened in Bath, whose hot springs had for centuries been associated with the Celtic goddess Sulis. The Romans made it a shrine to Minerva, their goddess of wisdom. But the earlier deity was still commemorated – she and Minerva in some way sharing their divinity. So much so that the place, which the occupiers built up into a major spa-centre, was given the name Aquae Sulis – 'Sulis's Springs'.

At Gosbecks Farm, near Colchester, Essex, excavations have revealed a temple consecrated to Camulos, a Celtic god who seems to have become identified with Mars, the Roman god of war. At Nettleton, in Wiltshire, meanwhile, the Romans took over a temple dedicated to Cunomaglus, the Celtic 'hound-lord', god of hunting, as a shrine to Apollo the Healer. The two deities were effectively fused together for those who worshipped here.

Some of these more offbeat devotions, though they may have been local in their origins, were nevertheless spread far and wide by the expansion of the Empire. (At the cutting edge of that expansion, the imperial army was especially cosmopolitan,

**BELOW: Based on the Olympian gods of the Greeks, the Roman pantheon provided a ready-made group of deities. Here we see Jupiter (the heavens), Neptune (the sea), Proserpina (agriculture), Pluto (the earth) and Salacia (Neptune's wife).**

LEFT: **Sulis Minerva represented a marriage of Roman and Celtic deities. She presided over the sacred springs in Aquae Sulis (Bath).**

drawing recruits from every corner of the Roman world.) One such cult was that of Cybele, the 'great mother goddess' of Anatolia (modern Turkey). She became associated with the Romans' own deity Ceres, goddess of the harvest, and is known to have had a following in Roman England.

Archaeologists working in London (the Roman Londinium) at the beginning of the twentieth century were astonished to unearth a first-century jug inscribed with a dedication to the Egyptian mother goddess Isis – who had a temple right next door, it said. A bronze figurine of Isis was subsequently found at Thornborough, in Buckinghamshire, suggesting that her adherents in England were, if not necessarily numerous, at least widespread. Shrines have been found along Hadrian's Wall to Mithras – an originally Persian god whose cult, with its emphasis on manly toughness and masonic secrecy, was particularly popular with soldiers. He too had a London shrine: the Mithraeum, in Walbrook, in the City.

Despite the best efforts of modern archaeologists, our understanding of these issues is still patchy at best. We don't know how these little sects took shape or how they rose and fell. Take Coventina, whose figurine was found in the remains of a well at Carrawburgh, near Hadrian's Wall. Although she is known to have been a Celtic water goddess and was clearly taken up by the Romans, we don't know if her cult was indigenous to Northumberland or if it was brought here by soldiers from Celtic lands on the continent.

## Of tiles and tales

It seems likely that the kind of complex intermingling that took place with religious influences also occurred with mythology at a local level – though, being at the local level, such stories didn't make it into the written record. Despite such variations, Romano-British culture was emphatically Roman overall. The higher you were in the social hierarchy, it seems probable, the more closely you would have identified with the overarching culture of the empire rather than the 'folk' traditions of the peasantry.

The stunning mosaics at Sussex's Bignor Roman Villa, for example, show figures from mainstream myths – the lovely Venus or the monstrous gorgon Medusa, for example. Ganymede, the

**BELOW: The Mithraeum, in Walbrook, London, was originally excavated in 1954, then moved to avoid being built over. It was returned to its original site in 2017.**

beautiful boy whom Jupiter carried off to be his cup-bearer is here, too. We see the god, in an eagle's form, sweeping him off to the summit of Olympus. Medusa also features in a floor at the Fishbourne Roman Palace, where we also see Venus's son Cupid riding on a dolphin.

It's a similar story at Chedworth where, appropriately, the floor of what was once a banqueting hall has a picture of Bacchus, the Roman god of wine and celebration, carousing with his sometime lover Ariadne. The daughter of Crete's King Minos, she is mostly famous for having helped save the Greek hero Theseus from her father's maze – and the Minotaur inside it. When Theseus subsequently abandoned, her, though, Bacchus found her easy prey.

Again, a sumptuous image, but one we might have found in any Roman villa from Spain to Syria. Its subject belongs to 'English mythology', maybe, but it's hardly what we'd understand as an 'English myth'.

## Boudica the Brave

Resistance to Roman rule in England was to continue sporadically – most notoriously in the rising of Boudica, warrior queen of the Iceni. Her husband Prasutagus, the historian Tacitus tells us, had tried to cooperate with the conquerors, but on his death his lands had been seized, his widow flogged and their daughters raped.

In 60–1, under Boudica's leadership, the Iceni rebelled, triggering a wider revolt, in the course of which the city of Camulodunum (now Colchester) was sacked. Londinium and Verulamium (St Albans) were also burned. By Tacitus' reckoning the rebels killed over 70,000 people (Romans and British) before they were brought up short by the legions of governor Gaius Suetonius Paulinus, who followed up their victory with general slaughter.

Not surprisingly, Boudica's memory endured – semi-mythic as it may have been. Again unsurprisingly, it was embraced with renewed enthusiasm in the reign of Queen Elizabeth I (1558–1603). And in that of Victoria (1837–1901), during whose time a celebrated statue – *Boadicea and Her Daughters* by Thomas Thornycroft (1815–85) – was erected in her honour beside the Thames.

## Roman reversals

We don't know what difference Christianization would have made to Roman England, its culture and mythology. The reality is that the Empire was already at or past its peak. Slowly but surely, it was to be in overall retreat from now. The Emperor Diocletian (c. 244–311; r. 284–305) had moved its western capital to Mediolanum (now Milan) in 286. That it had a 'western capital' at all was no doubt a testament to its size, but it also pointed to a tension that was eventually to bring it down.

**RIGHT: Venus, goddess of love, gazes up from the mosaic floor of the Roman villa at Bignor, Sussex.**

Power had increasingly become concentrated in the east, on Byzantium (now Istanbul). Constantine had made it his capital and named it (Constantinople) for himself. Rome was much weaker, though. The Sack of Rome by the Visigoths in 410 has come to be seen as a turning point. Understandably so: it was spectacular and traumatic. But its centrality in the popular historical consciousness has tended to obscure how long the Roman Empire had already been in decline by the beginning of the fifth century.

It had always been tough at the top in Rome. The first emperor, Augustus (63 BCE–14 CE; r. 27 BCE–14 CE) had himself seized power after a civil war. His own great-uncle Julius Caesar had been assassinated. That of Commodus (161–92; r. 176–92) was marred by conspiracies at court and ended with his assassination. And from then on, things never seem to have been quite the same. The constant turbulence took its toll. Though the state stayed strong, it increasingly lacked resilience (as modern psychologists would say). Once a sign of greatness, the vast extent of the empire started to seem like overstretch – the melting-pot of nations it ruled over no longer a measure of authority but a source of stress.

When the fifth century arrived, and with it a direct attack by a barbarian enemy, it was no longer in a position to defend itself. The Empire imploded, its legions withdrawn from the peripheries in a frantic effort to shore up imperial power at the centre – assailed not only by barbarian attack but by its own rivalries and dissensions.

## Cast adrift

In the case of England, the withdrawal of legions to help with the defence of Rome in the fifth century left its leading citizens feeling uncomfortably exposed. The defence of the realm appears to have been left (semi-officially) to an informal network of local warlords, whose chief loyalty was not to Rome but to themselves. Imperial rule may have been oppressive but it had at least been stable – not like the gangsterism that prevailed in England now.

Part no man's land, part every-man-for-himself land, the Roman province was increasingly beleaguered. Picts and Scoti carried out incursions into an undefended north. And, as the century wore on and Roman rule unravelled on the continent, Germanic tribesmen mounted speculative raids.

IN THE CASE OF ENGLAND, THE WITHDRAWAL OF LEGIONS TO HELP WITH THE DEFENCE OF ROME IN THE FIFTH CENTURY LEFT ITS LEADING CITIZENS FEELING UNCOMFORTABLY EXPOSED.

The Romans' retreat had been billed as a temporary measure but, as the years went by and the imperial centre continued to crumble, the prospect of the *Pax Romana* being renewed was evidently receding. The violent raids were the exception, not the rule: it's hard to know how nightmarish it was for most of the people most of the time. But it must all have felt deeply insecure. Above all, there was nothing to look forward to but an ever deeper spiralling into anarchy. Who was going to protect the people in the coming time?

A good question, and one that has never really had an answer. Not least because the identity of 'the people' was to be redefined. The Anglo-Saxons who formed the next 'invading' wave (again, it was all more complex and more gradual than that word makes it sound) were to acquire an honorary status as the original Englishmen and -women. In the modern mytho-history that has provided the popular view – and arguably informed the academic consensus rather more extensively than it should have done – the Anglo-Saxons were the 'real' ancestors of the English in a way that none of these other incomers could be.

# ANGLO-SAXON ADVENT

The idea of an 'English' nation really seems to have begun with the Anglo-Saxons. But with facts in short supply, mythology must take up the slack.

**OPPOSITE: Vortigern is smitten with the Saxon beauty Rowena in William Hamilton's painting of 1793.**

She looks the picture of innocence with her demurely downturned gaze, her long blonde tresses tumbling down her snow-white gown. How could such a fair frame contain anything other than a spotless soul? Who would guess at the evil in Rowena's heart? Certainly not Vortigern, the dark-haired Celtic chief who clutches at her hand, half-kneeling in his awestruck admiration of this Nordic beauty, begging to be placed beside her at the banqueting board that night.

## Mythic moments

William Hamilton (1751–1801), who painted this picture, specialized in scenes from Shakespeare, whose works were coming to be seen as quintessentially English at this time. But this work

OPPOSITE: **Hengist and Horsa arrive on the shores of Kent, in Vortigern's support, as imagined by the Anglo-Dutch antiquarian Richard Rowlands in 1605.**

BELOW: **Hengist sees off the Picts in this illustration from a fourteenth-century manuscript. That both sides here sport anachronistic chainmail reminds us that mythology is reinvented in every age.**

was one of a series he produced in 1793 to illustrate an edition of *The History of England* (by, ironically, the Scotsman David Hume, 1711–76). Certain episodes from history were becoming as iconic as anything on Shakespeare's stage.

They were probably about as factual; they were certainly as extravagantly stylized. According to the *Historia Brittonum*, this fair temptress was the daughter of Hengist, a Saxon chief who hoped to establish his own kingdom in southeastern England. She doesn't actually figure in the first account of the brothers Hengist and Horsa, which appears in the *Anglo-Saxon Chronicle* in the ninth century. The scribes who compiled this record content themselves with saying that, in the year 449, 'Hengest and Horsa, invited by Wurtgern, king of the Britons to his assistance, landed in Britain'. Vortigern, as the *Historia Brittonum* calls him, had invited the Saxon chieftains in to help him out against attacks by Pictish tribesmen from the north.

The king directed them to fight against the Picts, the *Chronicle* continues, and they did so; and obtained the victory wheresoever they came. They then sent to the Angles, and desired them to send more assistance. They described the worthlessness of the Britons, and the richness of the land. They then sent them greater support. Then came the men from three powers of Germany; the Old Saxons, the Angles, and the Jutes.

## Brothers grim

Little is known of the brothers Hengist and Horsa themselves. According to Hume, they possessed great credit among the Saxons, and were much celebrated both for their valour and nobility. They were reputed, as were most of the Saxon princes, to be sprung from Woden, who was worshipped as a god among those nations, and they were said to be his great grandsons; a circumstance which added

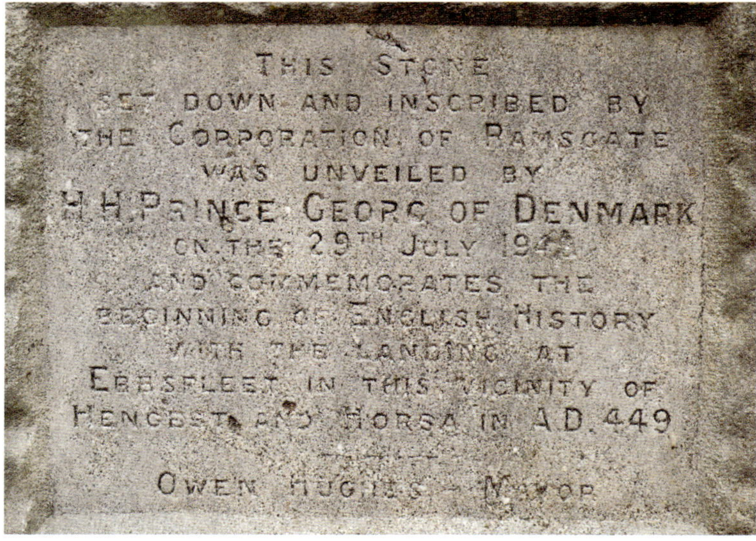


**ABOVE: A stone beside Ebbsfleet's Pegwell Bay marks Hengist and Horsa's landing there as 'the beginning of English history'.**

**OPPOSITE: Hengist explains to Vortigern why he has come to England. An illumination from a fourteenth-century French manuscript.**

much to their authority. As might be expected in one whose first fame was as a philosopher, and who was clearly conscious that he was writing in an 'Age of Reason', Hume shows a certain scepticism about such claims:

*We shall not attempt to trace any higher the origin of those princes and nations. It is evident what fruitless labour it must be to search, in those barbarous and illiterate ages, for the annals of a people, when their first leaders, known in any true history, were believed by them to be the fourth in descent from a fabulous deity, or from a man, exalted by ignorance into that character.*

An agglomeration of jostling, squabbling tribes, the Saxons had extended their power over much of western Germany, says Hume. Such was the competition between them for wealth and influence, however, that Hengist and Horsa had begun to look elsewhere. Hearing that the peoples of southern Britain were being beset by enemies from the north, they decided to go to England to lend a hand:

*They embarked their troops in three vessels, and about the year 449 or 450, carried over 1600 men, who landed in the isle of Thanet, and immediately marched to the defence of the Britons against the northern invaders. The Scots and Picts were unable to resist the valour of these auxiliaries; and the Britons, applauding their own wisdom in calling over the Saxons, hoped thenceforth to enjoy peace and security under the powerful protection of that warlike people.*

But then came the catch for Vortigern:

*Hengist and Horsa, perceiving, from their easy victory over the Scots and Picts, with what facility they might subdue the Britons themselves, who had not been able to resist those feeble invaders,*

*were determined to conquer and fight for their own grandeur, not for the defence of their degenerate allies. They sent intelligence to Saxony of the fertility and riches of Britain; and represented as certain the subjection of a people, so long disused to arms, who, being now cut off from the Roman empire, of which they had been a province during so many ages, had not yet acquired any union among themselves…*

*The Saxons in Germany, following such agreeable prospects, soon reinforced Hengist and Horsa with 5,000 men, who came over in seventeen vessels. The Britons now began to entertain apprehensions of their allies, whose numbers they found continually augmenting…*

Hume makes a point of explaining the Saxon takeover as a matter of what we would now call *realpolitik*, though he acknowledges that earlier writers preferred a more romantic tale. 'The love, with which Vortigern was at first seized for

**BELOW: A sixteenth-century engraving shows an Anglo-Saxon King attended on either side by his chief courtiers, with a row of what are supposed to be Germanic idols on the wall behind.**

Rowena, the daughter of Hengist, and which that artful warrior made use of to blind the eyes of the imprudent monarch.'

## Saxon seductress

For the full story we have to return to the pages of the *Historia Brittonum*, which talks us through Hengist's machinations in more detail. He 'prepared an entertainment', we're told,

> *...to which he invited the king, his officers, and Ceretic, his interpreter, having previously enjoined his daughter to serve them so profusely with wine and ale, that they might soon become intoxicated. This plan succeeded; and Vortigern, at the instigation of the devil, and enamoured with the beauty of the damsel, demanded her, through the medium of his interpreter, of the father, promising to give for her whatever he should ask. Then Hengist ... demanded for his daughter the province, called in English Centland, in British Ceint. This cession was made without the knowledge of the king, Guoyrancgonus who then reigned in Kent, and who experienced no inconsiderable share of grief, from seeing his kingdom thus clandestinely, fraudulently, and imprudently resigned to foreigners. Thus the maid was delivered up to the king, who slept with her, and loved her exceedingly.*

The first thing that strikes the modern reader in this twelfth-century passage, perhaps, is the number of enduring stereotypes that were already well-entrenched. Not just the age-old one of the femme fatale, but those of the rational Saxon and the undisciplined Celt, with his weaknesses for alcohol and emotion. A timely reminder of how important myths in this traditional

### Horses for courses

'Hengist' and 'Horsa' are Germanic words meaning 'stallion' and 'horse' respectively. Some scholars believe that they may originally have been twin equine deities, reduced to mortal status by Christian scribes – like the old Celtic gods.

The claim, reported by Hume, that they were believed to have been the grandsons of Woden would indeed have 'added much to their authority'. Woden was the great patriarch of the Germanic gods. (He was often depicted riding or accompanied by a horse – a mark alike of military prowess and social rank.)

Woden was associated with the sky, whereas his wife Frigg was associated with swamps and springs – she had her own wetland hideaway, a bog named Fensalir. They had a son together, Baldr (his son Brond was supposed to have been the ancestor of the kings of Anglo-Saxon Kent). Woden's most famous son, Thunor, whose mighty hammer was believed to make the sound of thunder, was borne by a mistress, the earth-mother Jorth. Another important member of the Germanic pantheon was Tiw, widely (but not universally) seen as a god of war. His relationship to Woden isn't clear.

sense can be in perpetuating myths of the more modern kind – widely held and insufficiently examined assumptions and beliefs.

**OPPOSITE: Rowena, in delicate déshabillé, passes yet another cup to the unsteady Vortigern. So (in mytho-history at least) are kingdoms lost.**

## Sources and sore points

In truth, though, we've really no reason to trust the hard-bitten shrewdness of Hume's narrative any more than we do the sensationalism of the *Historia Brittonum*'s. Much of the detail he adds to the *Anglo-Saxon Chronicle*'s account seems to have been drawn either from the *Historia Brittonum* itself or from Geoffrey of Monmouth's equally unreliable *History of the Kings of Britain*.

It's hard to know what would count as convincing testimony after so many centuries – during most of which time modern rules on academic rigour simply didn't hold. That even our medieval sources seem mostly to have been more or less embellished versions of the *Anglo-Saxon Chronicle* account doesn't inspire too much confidence. That account itself wasn't written until about four centuries after the events described, and it's hard to see it passing peer review today.

## Anglo-Saxon ascendancy

For what it's worth, though, those sources we do have agree that the Saxons came to Kent at the behest of a local chief or chiefs, essentially as mercenaries, but stayed, sensing an opportunity to take charge themselves. In the *Anglo-Saxon Chronicle*, things came to a head in 455, when Hengist and Horsa fought a pitched battle with Vortigern's forces at 'the place called Aylesford' (a village a few kilometres north of modern Maidstone).

Horsa, it says, was 'slain' there, though it doesn't actually tell us which side won the day. There's no ambiguity about the outcome of the Battle of Crecganford, two years later, though: 4000 Britons were killed and their force was put to flight from a field at Crayford (now an outer suburb of London, in the borough of Bexley).

In 460, we are told, the almost-certainly mythic Treachery of the Long Knives happened, when Hengist and his son Aesc called the Celtic chieftains to peace talks on Salisbury Plain, then ambushed and slew them all. The *Anglo-Saxon Chronicle* is silent on this, though it features in both the *Historia Brittonum*

**RIGHT: The Brittonic victory at Badon checked what until now had been an inexorable Saxon advance.**

and Geoffrey of Monmouth's *History of the Kings of Britain*. Almost as cruel, though, was the slaughter at Wippedesfleot (believed to have been Ebbsfleet, just south of Ramsgate), at which Hengist's men were claimed to have killed no fewer than 12 Celtic chieftains and many warriors.

The *Chronicle* continues with a catalogue of Saxon victories, which only ends with the defeat at Badon (or Mons Badonicus) in around 500. This victory is overlooked by the authors of the *Anglo-Saxon Chronicle*, though the Venerable Bede (c. 673–735), a Northumbrian monk, does have it in his *Ecclesiastical History of the English People*.

## An Anglo-Saxon heptarchy

Who were these incomers? We've seen that they included three peoples – Old Saxons, Angles and Jutes. Old Saxony at this time seems to have corresponded roughly with what is now known as Lower Saxony. The Angles came from the area more recently known as Schleswig-Holstein, which straddles the present-day border between Germany and Denmark.

The Jutes came from the Jutland Peninsula, now the mainland of Denmark. Each had their own identity, with their own traditions and beliefs. They did, however, share a broadly Germanic background and a commonality of purpose

## Sutton Hoo

A mound on level ground above the Deben estuary, near Woodbridge, Suffolk, turned out to be the site of a seventh-century ship burial. The ship itself – 27.5m (90ft) in length – had gone, its timbers rotted steadily away over so many centuries. But its imprint had been left in the enclosing earth. Inside lay the body of a man. He remains unidentified but, given the rich regalia and sumptuous weaponry and jewellery arrayed around him, he must have been of exalted rank. The many wonderful treasures included a decorative helmet, shield and sword and a richly ornate silver salver believed to have been brought from Byzantium.

Excavations over the years have uncovered a whole Anglo-Saxon cemetery, with some 20 prestigious barrows, built for wealthy chieftains. There was also an assortment of simpler, clearly much more humble graves. Like the ship, the bodies in these had disappeared – bones and all, eaten away by the acidity of the sandy soil – but they had left clear imprints behind them. Some had plainly been bound or twisted into tortured shapes, as though in punishment of some kind; others had quite clearly been beheaded.

**RIGHT: The Sutton Hoo Helmet underlines the wealth and power of the chieftain who once wore it and the sophistication of the Saxon civilization his burial represents.**

sufficiently strong for them to bond in opposition to their Romano-British foe.

When the fighting was done and the dust had cleared, they settled separate areas. The Saxons went to Essex in the east, to Sussex in the south and Wessex in the west – the names of these kingdoms reflected their association with the Saxons. Just as that of East Anglia did the region's settlement by Angles, though they also settled wide areas in Northumbria (literally, North of the Humber) and Mercia (the West Midlands, up against the Welsh border). Many of the Jutes settled down right where they'd landed, along the coast of Kent; others went to Hampshire and the Isle of Wight. The disposition and number of these Anglo-Saxon kingdoms changed as time went on. For the most part, though, they formed what is known as a heptarchy (rule of seven): East Anglia, Essex, Kent, Mercia, Northumbria, Sussex and Wessex.

As for what they were really like, what they believed or how they viewed the world, we're hampered by our lack of specific sources. Like the Celts, they seem to have avoided literacy themselves, so any contemporary writings about them were the work of outsiders (mostly Christian monks). Nowadays, too, we're handicapped as much as we're helped by the tantalizing similarities between the details available of early Anglo-Saxon culture and that of the Vikings (see next chapter), which is vastly better-known.

The parallels between their pantheon and that of the Norsemen are obvious – though it's clear that there were differences, at very least of emphasis, as well. The picture is complicated further by the fact that Anglo-Saxon attitudes were undoubtedly modified by their experience of life in England and by their contact with both Celtic and Christian cultural influences there. Indeed, modern academic experts see the descriptive 'Anglo-Saxon' as applying exclusively to the identity that took shape in the latter part of the first millennium in the English context.

**ANGLO-SAXON ATTITUDES WERE UNDOUBTEDLY MODIFIED BY THEIR EXPERIENCE IN ENGLAND.**

## The tree of life

We can really only guess how the Anglo-Saxons saw their cosmos as a whole. There's some evidence, though, that they saw it as being structured like a tree. We know that the Vikings were to speak of Yggdrasil, the 'life tree'. But the tradition ties in too with the evidence that the Celts honoured the oak tree, and held their ceremonies in sacred groves.

Indeed, trees appear to have been widely worshipped across all the ancient European cultures, the roots of this reverence apparently extending into a still more distant Indo-European past. As the landscape-historian Delia Hooke points out, the tree connects the earth, the realm of darkness and the dead, with the ground on which we walk in life and the heavens up above – not just the domain of the deities but the place from which the life-giving rain and sunshine come.

Its symbolic significance is to be detected in the biblical Book of Genesis, Hooke reminds us, while – topped as they are with foliate capitals – the columns of all those Greek temples are like so many stylized trees.

## From the pillar to the cross

Charlemagne (748–814; r. 768–814), king of the Franks and founder of the so-called Holy Roman Empire, fought a succession of wars against the Saxons in Germany. He was determined to convert them to Christianity, despite their frequently ferocious opposition. As a challenge, and as a gesture of intent, he began his first campaign in Paderborn, North-Rhine Westphalia, in 773, by destroying an Irminsul, the central symbol of the Saxons' pagan faith.

The word Irminsul means 'great pillar' in Old Saxon, and some of these idols do seem to have been made of stone. Mostly, though, they appear to have been wooden tree-trunks set up in open spaces, rather like the sort of standing stones seen at prehistoric henges.

**BELOW: Druids gather mistletoe from a sacred oak. The parasitic plant was believed to bring fertility.**

They were made of organic matter, though, so suggestive on the one hand of life and growth (their vaguely phallic air would have helped with this) and on the other of the death that they represented as they decayed. And, of course, they reminded worshippers of the tree of life and the way it connected the cosmos's different levels – the underworld, the realm of mortals and the sky.

Charlemagne's act of what he would have seen as sacred desecration would have sent the clearest of messages to the Saxons. In some ways, though, their old traditions were to prevail. The Anglo-Saxon poem *The Dream of the Rood* was

ABOVE: **Charlemagne's toppling of the Irminsul cleared the way for Christianity in Germany (in this early twentieth century reimagining). The Anglo-Saxons would be willing converts to the new religion.**

written in England, probably in much the same period – by which time the Saxons' kinsfolk in England were already overwhelmingly Christianized. In memorable terms, it describes the anonymous poet's experience of a vision in which he sees Christ's cross in the heavens, ablaze with light. He repeatedly describes it as a 'tree' – the 'victory tree' on which the Saviour won the world by giving up his own life in redemptive sacrifice; the special tree appointed to bear the Lord; and altogether a 'tree of glory'.

It's clear here that the word 'tree' is used to describe what we would call the wood from which the tree is made; just as a standing stone would be made with 'stone'. At the same time, though, the poem clearly makes the cross into an Irminsul of sorts – a uniquely Anglo-Saxon approach to the creed of Christ.

## Surrounded by spirits

Judaism, Christianity, Islam … the great monotheistic religions have been unanimous that 'God is everywhere', but believers still tend to see him as somehow existing at one remove. Up to a point, pagan societies have agreed with them. The Greek and

**ABOVE: On the south wall of the church in the village of Breedon on the Hill in Leicestershire stands this Anglo-Saxon carving of a lion.**

Roman gods were safely stowed away atop Olympus; the Vikings assigned their gods to a compound of their own at Asgard; there is even some indication that the Anglo-Saxons themselves believed in the existence of a *Hevenfelð* or 'Heavenly Plain'. Generally, though, it appears that pagans have expected to live at much closer quarters with the supernatural – whether to the ancestral spirits or to the divinities of meadows, springs or trees. Their more formal pantheons apart, the Greeks appeared to have believed that their homes were protected by ancestral spirits, the Romans that their homes were guarded by domestic deities, like the Lares and Penates. These beliefs seem to have belonged to older, more – for want of a better word – 'primitive' traditions: the classical pantheons became gradually more streamlined over time.

This sense of living in a spiritual environment saturated with supernatural presences appears to have been still more vital for the Celts; as it was for all those other peoples whose religious beliefs were based in animism – the belief that animals, places and natural features all have living essences in their own right.

Once the principle that the world about us resonates with life is accepted, it's but a short step to believing that all manner of less obvious living forms might exist as well. Giants, for example, or dragons – the Anglo-Saxons seem to have accepted their existence unhesitatingly.

## The Knuckerhole

A muddy pool in the corner of a muddy field outside the village of Lyminster in West Sussex has for centuries been said to be home to a 'knucker' – a monstrous water-dragon. In the story, the so-called Knuckerhole is bottomless; mundane measurement has found it to be only about 9m (30ft) deep, though this is still quite impressive for a village pond.

The knucker is believed to have got its name from the Old English nicor or water-wyrm (a 'worm' was what the Anglo-Saxons called a dragon, because it was essentially serpentine in form). Lyminster's knucker is one of several said to reside in similar stretches of open water the length and breadth of Sussex. They are liable to emerge at any moment and drag unwary passers-by beneath the surface.

**PAGANS HAVE EXPECTED TO LIVE AT MUCH CLOSER QUARTERS WITH THE SUPERNATURAL.**

One myth frequently begets another. That of Lyminster's Anglo-Saxon knucker gave rise to a succession of tall stories about local characters who hatched up their own ingenious ways of killing it. One Jim Pulk (or Puttock), a farmer's boy from nearby Wick, was said to have cooked the beast a specially poisoned pie. His plan worked perfectly – but then the hapless hero licked his fingers and died himself. A well-worn gravestone in the village church, known as the Slayer's Slab, is said to be that of the gallant medieval knight who killed it in a more romantic version of the tale.

## Elfin interference

The Anglo-Saxons also accepted the existence of the *aelfe* or elves who didn't just dwell in close proximity with mortal people but involved themselves more or less constantly in their lives. The aelfe don't appear to have been any different from ordinary

humans in their size. The idea that an 'elfin' form was small seems to be a modern one. Like the fairies later, the elves came back into the cultural mainstream literally diminished, as though to underline the fact that they represented a playful fancy rather than a real threat.

The *aelfe* certainly weren't the charming elves we think of now. Though they could do good, they were predominantly a force for ill. Quite literally in that, as Alaric Hall has shown, one of their most important functions in Anglo-Saxon life seems to have been that they were assumed to be responsible for sickness.

Understandably enough, perhaps: some explanation was required for why a robustly healthy individual might suddenly be seized by indisposition. Anglo-Saxon tradition attributed to malevolent elves what would in other pre-modern societies have been blamed on everything from witchcraft to miasmas (unhealthy mists).

Almost as unaccountable as illness, perhaps, is sexual desire. Aelfysce forces were seen as having the power to hijack the emotions and compromise the loyalties of the chastest or the truest. They came to maidens' beds by night and seduced them while they slept. Elfin women of enchanting beauty rejoiced in leading husbands from the straight and narrow. (This is presumably one reason why, when the elves were rehabilitated in modern times, they came back not just smaller but as comically old and ugly.)

These seductresses weren't wholly reliant on their looks, their insinuating style or sensuousness to score their conquests: they were adept in that form of magic known as *seithr*. Though in the first instance a form of divination – an ability to read the future, as ordained in an individual's *wyrd* or 'destiny' – it could all too easily shade over into the active manipulation of that person's fate.

Given the all but bewitching hold a beautiful woman was assumed to have over an unsuspecting man to begin with, it seemed more or less natural to see *seithr* as being particularly the property of female elves; though there were reports of male elves exploiting it as well.

**OPPOSITE: Elfin women were seen as seductive and manipulative in the most malevolent sense. They are much romanticized in this representation of 1882.**

## Willing converts

Talk of aelfysce influences continued long after the Anglo-Saxons had converted to Christianity, though exactly what was meant by such talk in this radically altered context is less clear. We don't in any case know clearly either when or why the Anglo-Saxons decided to be baptized. It wasn't because they had to, because their hold over England was secure. They would indeed have been well-placed to try to compel their Romano-British subjects to embrace the faith of Woden, Frigg and the rest, but they don't appear to have tried.

ABOVE: **Found on East Yorkshire's Holderness Peninsula, this seventh-century gold and garnet cross displays the prestige Christianity was coming to enjoy.**

It seems more likely that, proud though they were of their status as conquerors, they nevertheless sensed that they'd cast themselves in the barbarians' role. Christianity had clearly produced a comparatively glittering civilization in England: they wanted to belong to what seemed a sophisticated and forward-looking creed.

As we saw with the transition from the pillar to the cross, though, their Christianity did for a long time keep a distinctly Anglo-Saxon tinge. And aspects of the old beliefs appear to have endured as part of a rich and lively folklore.

## From water to fire

The idea of the nicor or 'water-wyrm', for instance. It has an odd, even counter-intuitive, ring to us today because our archetypal dragon is a scaly, four-footed creature that breathes fire – neither recognizably a worm nor in any way watery, in other words. In the most archaic traditions, though – as in Chinese folk-culture to this day – the dragon was indeed like a worm or snake in shape.

Or, to be more symbolically exact, an exaggerated phallus, its association with water embracing not just the fertilizing rain that allowed the crops to grow and feed us but the seminal fluid that enabled us to reproduce.

This ancient tradition took a turn somewhere in the Germanic past and so in Anglo-Saxon legend, along with the water-dwelling nicor, we start to find fire-breathing dragons of the now-conventional western kind.

In Freudian terms these monsters no longer seem to symbolize fertility, with its capacity to refresh and replenish, but the anally retentive urge to covet and possess, to close up, accumulate and hoard. Actually, the best-known dragon of this kind is probably J.R.R. Tolkien's Smaug, who lies in the midst of his mountain, jealously guarding his great mound of gold – but

## Reclaiming the Night

The solitary wayfarer stood rooted to the spot in fear: he might have been another tree in these remotest reaches of a deep, dark forest as, with a clamour of baying hounds, pounding hooves and sounding horns, they thundered past. A big but shadowy figure fled before; the pack pelted right behind him – the souls of the dead, the terrified traveller had heard it said.

The tradition of the 'Wild Hunt' has endured in several European cultures, but it has been particularly strong in Germanic ones. The folklorist Jacob Grimm (1785–1863) believed that it represented the survival of ancient pagan traditions. The hunt was led, he said, by Woden or his wife. As time went on and the hold of Christianity deepened not just on society and its institutions but on the imagination, the hunt was seen increasingly as a demonic force.

As with so much of the stuff of fairytale and folklore, modernity has been ambivalent in its attitudes, finding such stories simultaneously enjoyable and unsettling. That of the Wild Hunt serves as a reminder that, even if Christianity, civilization and order may rule the day, much darker spirits may have free rein once darkness falls.

**ASPECTS OF THE OLD BELIEFS APPEAR TO HAVE ENDURED.**

RIGHT: ***The Wild Hunt of Odin*, as imagined by the Norwegian painter Peter Nicolai Arbo (1831–92). As time went on and Christianity strengthened its hold across the Nordic nations, the pagan deities found a new imaginative function as demonic spirits.**

STRATHCLYDE
NORTHUMBRIA
BERNICIA
DEIRA
GALLOWAY
Lindisfarne
Tweed
Tyne
Jarrow
Durham
Tees
Whitby
Degsastan
x 603
Man
Swale
York
Wharfe
Heathfield
x 633
Humber
Manchester
LINDSEY
Lincoln
Dore
Trent
Chester
x 607 & 613
Faddiley
x 584
Nottingham
Derby
Maserfield
x 642
Stafford
MIDDLE ANGLES
Lichfield
Tamworth
Leicester
NORTH GYRWE
Stamford
SOUTH GYRWE
NORTH WALES
Severn
MERCIA
(MIERCE)
Bridgenorth
Warwick
Fen
Ouse
EAST ANGLES
St Edmundsbury
HWICCE
SOUTH ANGLES
Severn
Gloucester
Burford
Oxford
x 774
Hertford
EAST SAXONS
Witham
Ashdown
x 871
Bensington
x 777
MIDDLE SAXONS
London
Thames
Deorham
x 577
Englefield
x 871
Reading
x 871
Chippenham
Merton
x 871
Wedmore
Ethandun
x 878
Ockley
x 851
KENT
WESSEX
Ellandun
x 825
Winchester
Athelney
Wilton
x 871
Sherborne
SOUTH SAXONS
Wareham
Wight
WEST WALES
Hengests Dun
x 836
FRISIA

of course the author of *The Hobbit* (1937) had steeped himself in Anglo-Saxon lore.

**OPPOSITE: The Anglo-Saxon Heptarchy, according to this nineteenth century map.**

## Here be dragons

There was no shortage of Anglo-Saxon analogues, if we're to judge by certain modern English place-names. Those of the villages of Drakelow, Derbyshire, and Dragley, Furness, are both derived from the Old English phrase for 'dragon mound'.

Which takes us in turn to another odd fact. The Anglo-Saxons seem to some extent to have been spooked by their new surroundings in England. They appear to have found themselves haunted to some extent by features of its landscape and, in particular, to have sensed a certain menace in its monuments. They clearly knew that its barrows were burial sites, and were unsettled by the thought that so many strangers had preceded them so long before. The idea that dragons, wrapped around treasure hoards, had slumbered down the centuries in such mounds caught their imagination in a sometimes troubling way.

## Overawed

So too, however, had the signs that a great civilization had so recently extended its influence across their new English homeland, then suddenly withered right away. Some time towards the end of the first millennium, another anonymous Anglo-Saxon poet is believed to have walked wondering through what was left of Bath. A few centuries before, Aquae Sulis had been a grand and luxurious sacred spa. A magnificent baths complex had been built around the natural hot-water springs and a substantial settlement had slowly spread out across the surrounding hills.

In the space of a few generations, however, Aquae Sulis had gone to rack and ruin, its grandest monuments vandalized and raided for building-stone. Now flocks were grazed and livings scratched amid a collection of vast but dilapidated structures, whose provenance and purpose could only be guessed at. The poet's awestruck impressions were preserved in the *Exeter Book*, put together in the tenth century. They sum up his incomprehension in the face of so much ruined splendour:

*Wondrous is this wall-stone, dashed by destiny;*
*Battlements burst; the work of giants broken.*
*The roofs are ruined, the towers toppled,*
*The barred gate gone; the plaster frosted over,*
*The walls laid open, brought low, destroyed,*
*undermined by age …*

So far did this shattered shell of a city lie beyond the understanding of England's new inhabitants that it could be apprehended only quasi-mythically, as the work of giants. Its scale must have been daunting indeed to villagers living in small, thatched huts; so must its majestic arches and its stately colonnades. As 'The Ruin' makes clear, though, impressive as these constructions may have been, the destruction wrought by time was just as striking.

## A new England

But time could be constructive too. Indeed the 'Ruin' poet's incomprehension may well have been exaggerated; an attempt to

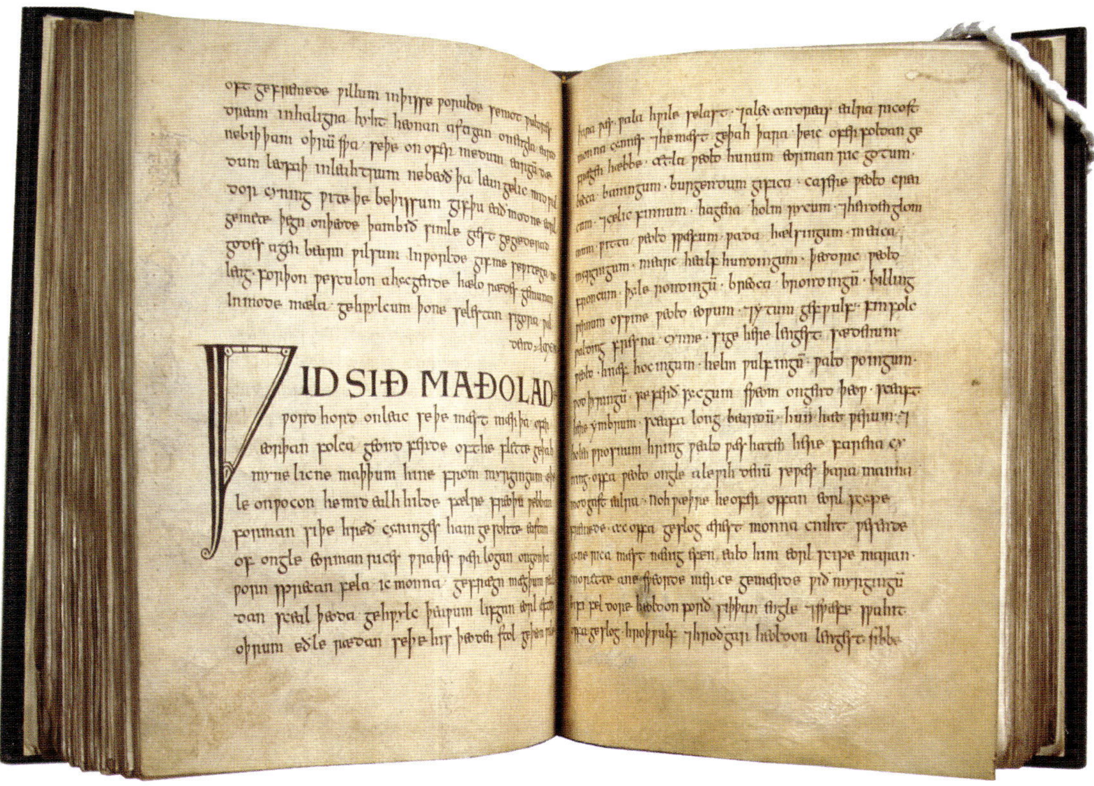


**BELOW: *The Exeter Book*, so-called because it was given to the library of Exeter Cathedral by its first Bishop, Leofric, in 1072, contains several classic works of Anglo-Saxon literature.**

gradually been disappearing. As, increasingly, had the collective memory of a prior, pagan life across the sea.

Their own memory was to live on, and in some unexpected ways, long after they themselves had been generally forgotten, however. The Anglo-Saxon era is intrinsically interesting, in so far as we can gain access to its culture and mythology. But it's fascinating too how its influence was to filter down through succeeding centuries.

## A SERMON IN A SPARROW

The circumstances of Edwin's conversion are reported by the Venerable Bede. The king had found the missionaries' message persuasive, but flinched from actually abandoning his old ways. He asked his advisers what they thought. 'Your majesty,' one said:

*...when we compare the present life of man on earth with that time of which we have no knowledge, it seems to me like the swift flight of a single sparrow through the banqueting-hall where you are sitting at dinner on a winter's day with your thanes and counsellors. In the midst there is a comforting fire to warm the hall; outside the storms of winter rain or snow are raging.*

*This sparrow flies swiftly in through one door of the hall, and out through another. While he is inside, he is safe from the winter storms; but after a moment of comfort, he vanishes from sight into the wintry world from which he came. Even so, man appears on earth for a little while; but of what went before this life or of what follows, we know nothing. Therefore, if this new teaching has brought any more certain knowledge, it seems only right that we should follow it.*

## A merry myth

It is now more than 400 years since Shakespeare wrote his captivating comedy *The Merry Wives of Windsor* (c. 1597), so it's an important period-piece in itself. It's intriguing, though, the extent to which the drama draws on even older Anglo-Saxon (and maybe even Celtic) mythic strands in fashioning a sophisticated entertainment for the Elizabethan age.

The play is utterly a drama of its own time in showing Windsor – famous, then as now, as a royal residence – as an emerging market town in which a new and prosperous middle class is on the rise. For the preposterous Sir John Falstaff – fat, vain and boastful; indeed devoid of any quality at all beyond his social status – Windsor's wives are nothing more than a tempting target.

Chronically short on funds, but long on self-esteem and entitlement, he's come to the town in hopes of snagging himself a wealthy married mistress to sponge off. But the Merry Wives see him coming and resolve that he'll be the one who's fooled.

OPPOSITE: **'Falstaff at Herne's Oak' by James Stephanoff (1787–1874). The Merry Wives prepare to bring the boastful, boorish, drunken knight down a peg or two.**

## Ancient rites

It's hard to see how the Anglo-Saxons could have been anything other than perplexed by the class comedy in Shakespeare's play: it satirizes social mores they'd have found unthinkably exotic. But they'd have enjoyed its rumbustious, slapstick humour – and, we can only imagine, felt the resonance it has in its darker, more serious moments of a night-time world of mystery and dream. And of a half-remembered pagan past that can make a midnight forest into a sacred grove, a place of powerful magic – and of an oak tree under which human sacrifices are made.

Mistress Page may be mocking that tradition when she invokes the story of Herne the Hunter. It's in his guise that Falstaff must go into the woods that night, she says. To do that, he must first don decorative antlers (a pagan symbol, she plausibly enough implies but to Shakespeare's audience the headgear of the comic cuckold). Once he's there, she and her friends will be able to meet him without their husbands knowing. Her plan is to send some village children dressed as fairies to scare Sir John out of his wits, but the whole scheme will depend on ancient atmospherics for its success. 'There is an old tale goes,' she says, 'that Herne the Hunter,'

*Sometime a keeper here in Windsor forest,*
*Doth all the winter-time, at still midnight,*
*Walk round about an oak, with great ragg'd horns;*
*And there he blasts the tree and takes the cattle*
*And makes milch-kine yield blood and shakes a chain*
*In a most hideous and dreadful manner:*
*You have heard of such a spirit, and well you know*
*The superstitious idle-headed eld*
*Received and did deliver to our age*
*This tale of Herne the hunter for a truth.*

It may be the stuff of superstition, put about by the 'idle-headed eld' – old fools, in other words – but it's clearly still culturally current to some degree. And, of course, it now has everlasting standing as literature in a classic work by England's greatest poet.

# BEOWULF

England's first epic poem isn't actually set in England, but it lays down the law on what was to be expected of an English leader.

The greatest poem of the Anglo-Saxon age describes the feats of a hero who's otherwise unknown, though his story brushes up against a number of other narratives (a few of them thought to be historical) of the time. Beowulf, he's called. His name, it's widely believed, translates as 'wolf of bees' – a poetic way of saying 'bear' – but some scholars have suggested a derivation from *beado wulf* or 'wolf of war'. Either way, as a boy he was effectively left an orphan, his father having been exiled for a killing at home among the Geats of southern Sweden and forced to seek a sanctuary abroad.

Beowulf, however, had grown to heroic manhood, a 'thane' or trusted retainer of Hygelac, the Geatish king. 'Far did his fame fly', as fighter, as leader of men and as adventurer at sea. So it

**OPPOSITE: Grendel stands for all that is dark and frightening in the Anglo-Saxon mind.**

should be for any lord, the poem's prelude breaks off to say. He should make it the purpose of his life to bring home booty. Then, when he dies, his men in mourning can gently place him in his ship and set him adrift for one last voyage across the empty, ice-curdled sea.

## Where the hart is

Hrothgar, the poem's narrator continues – abruptly switching settings – had led just such a life of honour and success. Although he came from a line of Danish kings, the so-called Scyldings, he had earned his renown and won his following by his warlike prowess and his personal charisma. His courage in combat was equalled only by his generosity in sharing out the spoils; his scrupulousness in honouring his word.

**THE HALL WAS THE CENTRE OF HEROIC LIFE – THE BEATING HEART OF EXISTENCE FOR THE SORT OF SUPER-MILITARIZED MALE.**

So great a warband did Hrothgar assemble that he had to build himself a mighty mead-hall to house them in. It was richly appointed, its roof and walls trimmed out with gold. He named it 'Heorot' – the name means 'hart' or 'stag' (a sacred animal and a royal one in Germanic tradition) – and it is believed to have been at Lejre, not far from Denmark's northern Zealand coast.

The hall was the centre of heroic life – the beating heart of existence for the sort of super-militarized male who is the main protagonist and presumed listener for ancient epic. The 'Wanderer' who laments his exiled plight in the famous Anglo-Saxon poem of that name, says he's *seledreorig* – 'sad in hall-lessness'. He's homesick – but not for what we would probably see as a 'home'. It isn't the comfort of the hearth he misses – still less the embrace of a loving wife – but the generosity and trust of his beloved lord and the warmth and camaraderie of his fellow warriors.

It's all about 'male-bonding', in other words.

*He recalls hall-companions*
*the handing out of treasure;*
*how in his youth*
*his lord, his gold-friend*
*got him used to banqueting.*
*All that joy has died.*

Homer's heroes would have recognized these feelings; so would Virgil's Aeneas. They'd have recognized the elegiac tone, as well. The epic idiom is arguably intrinsically nostalgic: the age of true heroism is always in the past. If Homer's *Iliad* harks back wistfully to an age when men were men, his *Odyssey* is explicitly the story of a hero's efforts to find his way home from the war to his ancestral hall. Virgil's *Aeneid* openly aches for the noble simplicity of the age imperial Rome is seen as having left behind.

Hrothgar's Heorot was just this kind of hall – not just a 'massive mead-house,/ greater than ever yet seen by the sons of the earth', but a place of welcome and belonging for his men. The kind of welcome and belonging that, it's implied, is no longer to be had. That *Beowulf* is shot through with nostalgia too becomes clear almost immediately, when the peace and order of this manly paradise are overturned.

**BELOW: The entire ethos of *Beowulf* is based on the idea of a brotherhood of warriors loyal to their chief. Halls like this (at Jarrow, England) were central to this way of life.**

## From merrymaking to massacre

Evil irrupts in the form of Grendel, monster of the mere. While he undoubtedly embodies an ancient pagan fear of 'marsh and moor,/of fen and wilderness', Grendel is given a Judaeo-Christian pedigree of evil, too. The poem is explicitly set in pagan times, but in hindsight with what its narrator plainly feels is the advantage of a Christian perspective. Grendel was, we're assured, one of that host of giants, elves

**ABOVE: Cain's killing of his brother Abel has haunted the human consciousness as the archetypal act of violent betrayal. Here it is imagined by Paolo Guidotti (1560–1629).**

and demons spawned by Cain, that son of Adam and Eve who murdered his brother Abel in the Bible (Genesis 4).

This is just the first of many biblical references made by an author who may also have known a number of the Latin classics. There's no doubt that, like the Irish epics, *Beowulf* was at very least written down by a Christian monk. Some scholars believe that *Beowulf* was originally a pagan epic given a rough-and-ready Christian makeover by this scribe; others have seen its Christianity as integral to the text.

Either way, it lends itself to a comparatively deep and thoughtful reading. *Beowulf* is no gung-ho comic strip. Grendel wasn't just a monster of malevolence (though he was that): he was also very clearly a tormented soul. Confined to the dark depths of the water as though in his own individual hell, he heard the distant racket from their revelry and was filled with 'anger and envy'. He heard not just the noise of feasting but the sound of the strumming harp and the song of the bard recounting the story of God's creation of the world – its lands; its seas; its skies; its sun and moon. We're left uncertain whether he most resented his exclusion from this perfect cosmos or his outsidership vis-à-vis the world of men. Whichever it was, the note of empathy takes us by surprise.

Grendel himself had no compassion, though. Stealing from his swamp one night in the small hours, after the joyful hubbub of the feast had subsided, he made his way into Heorot and saw Hrothgar's sleeping men. They'd been boozing and gormandizing and – the narrator frets with striking (and strikingly Christian) scrupulousness – hadn't had the chance to confess these sins and receive the absolution of a priest. So it was particularly cruel that it should be at just this point that Grendel should reach out and help himself to a handful of 30 and make off back to the mere with them. It wasn't until dawn a few hours later when the company awoke that they were missed. 'Then after feasting were lamentations raised.'

## 'HWAET! …'

'Lo!', 'Look!', 'Listen!', 'Hearken!', 'Pay heed!' ... However you translate it, the first word of *Beowulf* arrests the reader's attention – just as it once cut through the hubbub of a crowded, noisy hall. So we're invited to imagine, at least. The assumption with heroic epics such as those of Homer has always been that they were delivered vocally; declaimed to rough, tough, raucous warriors as they sat and drank.

How far that was ever actually true we have to wonder. Wasn't the declamatory style more about establishing atmospherics for a more sober hearer in a quieter and more intimate setting? It works that way for the reader embarking on the poem privately today, but we don't know how likely it is that anyone would have attempted to approach it that way in the eighth century, when it's believed it was composed. Historians aren't sure that what we think of as 'reading' – silently, inwardly, in the comfort of an armchair or maybe at a desk – really came in before the advent of the mass-market novel in the eighteenth century.

Virgil's *Aeneid* very clearly makes a performance of being a heroic epic, but it seems too densely 'literary' to have been taken in by hearers in any hall. It's the same with *Beowulf* – along with all its warlike-sounding exclamations, and its often thrilling action scenes, it's self-consciously learned, and very highly wrought. *Beowulf* has the additional aim, it's clear, of coming up with a Christian approach to heroic action; of reconciling the warlike glamour of the old ways with the path of peace.

## Hall of death

The next night, Grendel was back for more. And the one after; and the one after that … The monster followed his feud against Hrothgar's hall and evil reigned. Picking off travellers, high and low, as they made their way across local moorlands, he brought social and economic life to a complete standstill. He, not Hrothgar, was now the Lord of Heorot.

Through 12 long years the persecution went on. Hrothgar and his close advisers tried every tactic they could think of for freeing their land from the monster's depredations, but all in vain. They asked the help of their deities, making offerings at every heathen shrine they could think of. They didn't know 'Lord God' himself, nor the protective 'helmet' of his heaven, the narrator says. (There's an inconsistency here – or, as we'd say in modern times, some 'poetic licence' being used. We saw the bard singing the praises of a Christian creation above: it suits the author now for us to see Hrothgar and his people as still pagans because it points up their helplessness in the face of Grendel's gruesome attentions.)

**THEY DIDN'T KNOW 'LORD GOD' HIMSELF, NOR THE PROTECTIVE 'HELMET' OF HIS HEAVEN.**

## The adventurer arrives

Eventually, word of Heorot's sufferings reached Beowulf in southern Sweden where, though yet a thane of Hygelac, he was held in high account, acknowledged 'great among the Geats'. He asked his lord for permission to prepare a ship so he could make his way across the 'swan-road' (the sea) to Heorot and help free Hrothgar from his evil curse. Taking with him 14 of Hygelac's boldest men, he set sail, his vessel skipping over the waves like a bird with a breast of foam until on the second morning they sighted land.

When they reached the shore, they were challenged by a sentry, who praised their purpose and promised to take them to Hrothgar. Stunning as ever, his hall shone bright with gold as they approached. Inside, however, its lord presented a very different and more dismal picture, white-haired and old, bowed down with age and grief. Even so, he welcomed the heroes graciously – as he did Beowulf's eloquent offer of help in his despair. He had, he acknowledged, known and respected the young man's father.

Sadly, Hrothgar reflected on what grim work Grendel's hatred had wrought on him and his hall over these past 12 years. Many of his mightiest warriors had bravely tried to protect his home and his community. The monster had duly snatched them all

**LEFT: Hrothgar, aged by his sufferings, welcomes Beowulf to Heorot. He hardly dares hope that the young warrior can save his people.**

away. Even so, he would not neglect his hostly duty to the newcomers, inviting them all to sit and feast with him that night.

## Fight or flyte?

For a few hours that evening, as the daylight slowly ebbed away outside, it was as though the monster's rage had never been. The beer flowed, the conversation, the laughter rose.

As did Hrothgar's henchman Hunferth, with needling comments to be made about Beowulf's inability to live up to his heroic self-presentation. He reminded him of the swimming-match he reportedly lost against his boyhood friend Breca. He was 'envious', we're told, though modern scholars have speculated that, given the importance of the occasion and of this particular guest to Hunferth's lord, his attack is more likely to have been an example of the 'flyting' – scathing but stylized insults – exchanged by epic heroes by way of banter.

**THE GREATEST OF THE 'WORMS' HAD GRIPPED BEOWULF'S BODY AND DRAGGED HIM DOWN TO THE DEPTHS BEFORE HE COULD FREE HIMSELF AND RUN IT THROUGH WITH HIS SWORD.**

Beowulf was unperturbed: the interruption allowed him to describe in detail how, armed with swords against attacks by whales, he and Breca did indeed set out to race across the strait between the island of Brännö and the Finnish mainland. Breca had been well beaten when they were attacked by nicors (see 'Knuckerhole' in chapter 1). Beowulf had engaged them, allowing Breca to make his escape. The greatest of the 'worms' had gripped Beowulf's body and dragged him down to the depths before he could free himself and run it through with his sword. He'd slain nine of these horrible sea-serpents in all. Had Hunferth been as valiant as his battle-boast makes out, Heorot would never have been in such a plight, he added.

All laughed, and Hrothgar's queen Wealhtheow personally brought Beowulf a cup of mead to welcome him and his men and thank them for their assistance. The feasting continued into the early hours. Finally, as he stood up to leave and take himself off to his lordly lodgings to sleep, Hrothgar hailed his young visitor and wished him luck. Never before had he entrusted his hall to any man as he did now to Beowulf.

## Duel in the dark

The royal party retired and Beowulf and his men settled themselves down in the dark and silent hall to await the monster's arrival, the hero trusting in his own strength and courage and in God's support. So much so, indeed, that he took off his armour and his helmet, and even laid aside his trusty shield and sword before he settled down to sleep. He'd tackle his foe bare-handed, he said, without relying on his weaponry: 'Let the Lord decide our contest as he sees fit.' Beowulf showed all the valour and the warlike trappings of the pagan, epic hero, but ultimately his courage was Christian – a calm submission to God's will.

All but one of the warriors slumbered as the 'shadow-walker' strode through the pallid night, towards the hall. Beowulf waited wakeful, to face his foe. Grendel saw the shape of the hall, its fittings glinting as he approached its door. He shattered the heavy

**LEFT: Beowulf's warriors try to help their lord, but their sword- and spear-points bounce harmlessly off the monster's hide.**

bolts with a single blow and rushed inside. He grasped a sleeping form, bit through it and drank its blood down in a gulp. As he reached for a second figure, though, he was himself seized, his arm held hard and fast by far and away the most powerful grip he'd ever felt. Overcome with fear, he tried to tear himself away, to flee back to his fen.

But Beowulf would not let go, however violently Grendel wrestled with him and heaved and tugged and scrabbled to get away. The Geatish warriors were awoken by the crashing din and stared, bewildered, to see their chieftain thrashing about in his death-struggle with their monster. Recovering their composure, they gathered about and thrust at Grendel with their swords, but their blades couldn't hurt a hide that had the protection of wicked spells.

It didn't matter. Beowulf held fast to his arm, and though Grendel did eventually tear himself free, he left his whole arm – from the hand to the shoulder – behind in the hero's clutches. Bleeding fast, the monster knew that he was as good as dead, but even so he hoped to reach the security of his home in the dark depths of the mere before the spirit left him. He left Beowulf and his band rejoicing. They mounted Grendel's arm, still steaming, on the wall of Heorot as a trophy. They would toast it, and their leader's victory, that night.

**BELOW: With the strength of 30 men, Beowulf tears Grendel's arm off at its socket. The monster will manage to creep home, but has been mortally wounded.**

## Happy Heorot

People came from far and wide to see the torn-off limb in Hrothgar's hall. Its nails had the look of tempered steel. Some of the men tracked Grendel's gory steps to the edge of the mere, and gazed wonderingly into its boiling, blood-frothed waters. Joy was unconfined and Beowulf's deeds held up for admiration: before the day was done it was the subject of stirring song. Hrothgar came to Heorot himself, gave thanks and praise to Beowulf for what he had achieved and promised from that day on to love him as a son. That night's feasting was more joyous and more boisterous than it had ever been before. The bard entertained them all with a heroic account of Hrothgar's great ancestor Healfdene and his raid against the Frisians. Again, Wealhtheow drank Beowulf's health.

Finally, after many hours, the company grew tired, the mood subsided, the royal couple left – as did Beowulf, who'd been given his own separate accommodation – and the weary warriors lay down to rest. Soon they were sleeping peacefully, the burden of anxiety at last removed from those who had lived in fear for a dozen years.

**ABOVE: Having followed the trail of blood, Beowulf finds Aschere's head on the bank of the deep, dark mere – left there by Grendel's mother as she fled.**

## A mother's vengeance

Their ease was premature. Grendel's mother had lost her beloved son and was bent on cruel revenge. She made her way, in her late child's footsteps, to Hrothgar's hall. Smaller and weaker than her son, as woman is to man, she felt fearful but was desperate for vengeance. She found her way into Heorot, grabbed a sleeping man and dashed away.

The warrior she'd seized was Aeschere, one of Hrothgar's closest comrades and most trusted counsellors. His loss came as a hammer-blow to a king who'd thought his years of endless mourning were now done. But Beowulf, arriving now and hearing what had happened, told him not to sorrow: it was far better to avenge his friend than mourn him.

Hrothgar, Beowulf and their remaining men set off on the mother-monster's trail. Together they tracked her back to the water's edge. There on the bank was Aeschere's head. The sea below seethed red with blood; serpents swam among the waves and nicors lay up along the shore, but they scattered at the sound of Hrothgar's war-horn.

## Down to the depths

Undaunted, Beowulf put on his chainmail coat and his wonderfully worked helmet, with boar-head decorative flourishes to ward off sword-strokes. Hunferth, his earlier quarrel forgotten, gave Beowulf his own sword, an heirloom, tempered in blood and never known to have let its wielder down in battle. Asking Hrothgar to look after his men if he should not resurface, Beowulf set off into the waves and was lost to view.

**THE SEA BELOW SEETHED RED WITH BLOOD.**

It took him most of the day to reach the bottom of the mere, but once he got there, Grendel's mother lost no time in coming out to meet him. He swung his sword, but though it played a battle-song upon her head, it would not bite; he tried again and once more it glanced harmlessly off that accursed hide. Throwing aside his sword, he decided to trust to the strength that had seen him through against Grendel just the day before. He grabbed his assailant, and threw her to the floor. She quickly recovered, reached for him and dragged him down into some deep, strange chamber in which, by some enchantment, it was dry and fires burned. Ready to deliver the coup de grâce, the monster-mother whipped out a long knife. Swinging savagely, she tried to stab him through the breast with its burnished blade. But God placed the mail in its murderous path and he was saved.

Rising to his feet, he saw, glowing in the firelight, a magic sword. He seized it and ran the monster through. As she crumpled to the floor in death, Beowulf saw her son. He took his sword and cut off his head to show to Hrothgar. Blood gushed forth and rose up through the waters – the watching warriors above saw, and feared for their hero. He, meanwhile was watching in disbelief below as the blade of the sword he'd used to decapitate Grendel melted away before his eyes, apparently destroyed by the action of the monster's blood.

## Back to life

Above, on the banks of the mere, as time went by and no Beowulf appeared, Hrothgar and his men gave up the wait and went off disconsolate. Beowulf's own men, on the other hand, wouldn't leave. They hoped against hope to see their lord once more. Their faith was finally rewarded when he broke the surface, gasping and spluttering, holding out the head of Grendel and the hasp of his now-ruined magic sword.

**LEFT: Beowulf seized the sword and cut off the slain Grendel's head to show to Hrothgar. Blood gushed forth and floated to the surface of the mere.**

Happily, they helped their leader ashore. They took Grendel's head – it needed four men to carry it – and set off back to Heorot to show their hosts. All stared in amazement as they bore in the grisly trophy. Beowulf showed Hrothgar the hilt of what had hours earlier been a sword and told him how he with his courage – and the help of his heavenly Lord – had won the day. Hrothgar gave his thanks both to Beowulf and God.

## A heroic homecoming

Laden with gifts and gratitude, the adventurers set off on their voyage back to Geatland. They were given a heroes' welcome in their home. Hygelac was as appreciative of what Beowulf had done as Hrothgar himself was. All won when the code of honour was upheld.

The years went by and Beowulf gave his lord his full support. Finally, though, Hygelac fell in the field of war. Beowulf became his successor – and a noble one, reigning for 50 years over what was a happy and prosperous realm. One peril lay in wait, though – literally lay, a dragon sleeping through long centuries in its mound atop a hoard of gold and jewels and other treasure, a relic of now-distant heathen times.

The mound rose up high above the sea in a wasteland that received few visitors. One day, however, a fugitive fleeing from

## Scribal censorship or Christian classic?

Poems such as *Beowulf* were written down by Christian monks, as we've seen. The monks' influence is clearly evident in the texts they produced. Not just in the many biblical allusions but in bigger, broader areas of symbolism and structure. Take Beowulf's descent into the depths of the mere, his death-struggle down there with Grendel's mother and his triumphant return to daylight and air … These bring obvious echoes of the medieval tradition of Christ's 'Harrowing of Hell'.

This was the belief that, in the three days through which his body lay in the tomb, after his crucifixion on Good Friday, Jesus went in purpose down to the underworld to break down Satan's gates and release those virtuous souls who'd been confined there, having died during the pagan era, condemned by the 'original sin' of Adam and Eve before humankind had been redeemed by Christ's suffering and death.

Beowulf's final battle with the dragon would of course be an exciting, all-action fight to the death. But it was also clearly a Christ-like act of self-sacrifice. The hero accepted his death as the price of his people's salvation from demonic terror.

For some modern scholars, *Beowulf* has been self-evidently a pagan work, tinkered with at the edges by the Christian scribes who wrote it down. An appealing take, in a romantic way, but how convincing is this really? And in any case, how interesting is it by comparison with the view that this was a sort of Anglo-Saxon *Aeneid*? That is, the big and complex epic of a new and forward-looking (if in some ways obviously nostalgic too … ) but above all buoyantly self-confident civilization?

**OPPOSITE: In the 'Harrowing of Hell', the dead Christ descended to the underworld to free the unredeemed souls in Satan's captivity there.**

## An 'oral' aesthetic?

Anglo-Saxon poetry doesn't rhyme; nor does it scan by syllables the way that modern English does. Rather, it lurches along from alliteration to alliteration ('Hrothgar, happy in his hall …'; 'the shadow of death hunted him down in darkness … '). It's a system that lends itself to the declamatory style of the bard at the banquet, making himself heard over the hubbub of talking, laughing men and clattering utensils.

So too does the use of repetition – of what are already formulaic phrases and stock epithets (the sea as 'the swan's path' or 'the whale's way'; a sword as a 'battle-blade'; a bloody hero as 'sword-gore-stained' … ). These would be marked down as cliché in modern verse. To the audience listening in a crowded hall, though, the use of such familiar material would make it easier to keep track, while simultaneously 'placing' the poem's action in an august canon of heroic tales. So, too, do apparently digressive stories such as that of Beowulf and Breca's swimming race and Healfdene's conflict with the Frisians.

But all these elements had an additional purpose in facilitating the work of a bard who had to be able to turn out epic poetry by the yard. Research into the storytelling traditions of a great many pre-literate cultures has revealed widescale reliance on ready-made formulas of this kind. Not just of imagery or language, indeed, but of narrative, too – chunks of storyline that can be introduced to spin out a longer tale – without taxing the memory of the bard too much.

As we've seen, there's reason to suspect that most of the ancient epics we know were works of nostalgia. They harked back to a lost heroic age, rather than representing one. They weren't the authentic record of anything that was actually performed for feasting warriors. How much that matters is another question. They clearly are authentic records of the ancient cultures that produced them – even if those cultures turn out to have been more troubled in their attitudes, more ambivalent in their feelings, than may first appear. And, as we see in *Beowulf*, they work. They evoke the atmosphere of the mead-hall in all its epic masculinity and excitement.

the authorities and seeking a place to hide stumbled on a previously secret entrance into the hillside. Within he saw the glow of gold; he grabbed a goblet and fled in mingled fear and glee.

With the morning, the dragon woke. He immediately sensed that an intruder had violated his stronghold. Despite the rich abundance of his hoard, he could tell a cup had gone astray. He waited, his incandescent rage contained but quietly building in his wrathful heart till evening descended and darkness came.

### Flames and fury

He burst forth from his fastness, exhaling flames and casting a lurid glow across the sky from horizon to horizon, burning homesteads and bringing destruction far and wide. He even burned down Beowulf's hall. Much to that hero's fury. Beowulf and his warriors tried to fight off the dragon's attack but failed. The sun rose instead upon a blackened, smoking ruin.

Beowulf, both angry and sad, gathered 11 of his strongest warriors around him and set off with them to find the dragon's mound.

The malefactor who took the goblet went along to guide them. Fittingly, since he'd caused them all so much trouble, he made a thirteenth man. He took them to the headland and they climbed to the very entrance of the dragon's lair, before Beowulf bade them halt and gather round to hear his words.

ABOVE: Anglo-Saxon ideas of natural history were as extravagant as they were uninformed. This bestiary was bundled in with the manuscript of *Beowulf.*

## Facing death

His address to his most trusted retainers has something of the character of a farewell. His mood seemed thoughtful, downbeat, death-expecting. He'd had a long life, he acknowledged, with its share of struggles – he recalled some highlights here. But now it was time for him to face his fate. He would, he insisted, go into the dragon's den alone, unflinching. One fight would settle his feud with this fiery monster; his destiny would decide whether he'd prevail. Although he'd prefer to go in unarmed as he did against Grendel – and, ultimately, his mother – he had to contend with the flames the dragon breathed, so would take his sword and wear his iron corselet and coat of mail.

Into the entrance-passage he stepped; into the bowels of the earth where the wyrm wound itself around its hoard and hissed in fury, spitting sparks and snorting deadly flames at his

approach. Swinging his sword, the hero struck. His blade sank through scales and scabrous flesh but bent slightly, its sharp edge flattened, as it hit the bone. As every man must one day when at life's end, Beowulf found himself facing his maker, for final judgement; he had to confront his fate alone. Already, though, he was groggy with the heat and weakened by his wounds.

**OPPOSITE: With Wiglaf's assistance, Beowulf beats off the attack of the fire-breathing dragon in what is destined to be his final triumph.**

## A friend in need

One alone of his comrades had refused to heed his lord's orders to absent himself and had followed him hesitantly down the passage, pushing deep into the mound. Believed to be Beowulf's nephew, Wiglaf serves a more symbolic role as well. His name, fittingly, means 'vestiges of valour'. The parallel between Beowulf and Jesus here is obvious. As is the 'coincidence' of his having brought 12 men to witness his suffering and death. Wiglaf is a sort of anti-Judas, the only one to remain completely loyal. Appearing suddenly through a haze of blood and smoke, he struck at the dragon with his own sword, fighting bravely alongside his uncle.

**THE PARALLEL BETWEEN BEOWULF AND JESUS HERE IS OBVIOUS.**

Enraged at this interference, the dragon turned with a roar and a torrent of flames. Wiglaf's help had only made their situation still more dangerous, it seems. But, as the dragon coiled round to sink its noxious fangs into Beowulf's neck, Wiglaf managed to stab him with his sword. The startled monster relaxed his hold for a brief moment. The reprieve gave Beowulf the time he needed to grab his dagger and cut the dragon clean in half.

Once more, Beowulf had been victorious. This was without doubt his final triumph, though. The dragon's bite was venomous. He could feel his body being corroded from within. As his supporters stole timidly into the chamber, Wiglaf upbraided them for their cowardice. It hardly mattered now, though: by this time their lord lay as good as dead. His last request was that his people raise a barrow for him on a headland above the sea, where brave men would see it as they returned home from their raids. And so stands the poem Beowulf itself, a memorial not just to a mythic hero but to the heroic values of an age.

# DANISH DOMINATION

Paradoxically, the Vikings helped to build the England they so assiduously raided and invaded – if only by giving it something to define itself against.

OPPOSITE: **The Great Heathen Army attacks Thetford, Norfolk, as seen – and stylized – by a monastic scribe in the illuminated *Life of Edmund* (c. 1130).**

'From the fury of the Northmen, Lord deliver us … ' went the prayer offered up in Europe's monasteries. On the night of 8 June 793, he hadn't, though. For it had been then that, according to the *Anglo-Saxon Chronicle*, 'the ravages of heathen men' had 'miserably destroyed God's church on Lindisfarne, with plunder and slaughter.'

Lindisfarne, a tidal island off the coast of Northumberland, northeast England, was famed for its abbey, revered the length and breadth of Christendom for the value of its treasures and the learning of its monks. So it hadn't just been a terrible attack, but a symbolic blow struck at Christianity. To the pagan Vikings, monasteries were always a tempting target, offering golden chalices, splendid vestments, precious books and other

The reconstructed tenth-century settlement at Bork, West Jutland, gives a vivid impression of the kind of places England's Danish invaders came from.

**OPPOSITE: Already established as a king in Russia, Oleg of Novgorod in 907 led a Viking army against the might of Constantinople.**

treasures. And their inhabitants were more used to peaceful prayer than fighting.

These Scandinavian 'sea wolves' struck without warning – generally just one or two longships at a time, but with the advantage of surprise and sheer ferocity they invariably prevailed. Setting fire to houses, sacking churches, seizing valuables and captives and driving off livestock, they would be back on board ship and off to sea before any serious resistance could be organized.

## Anglo-Saxon spin

It's a measure of how far popular history has come that it considers the Anglo-Saxons as a sort of default 'English' population and the Vikings are invariably 'othered'. In truth, as we've seen, the Anglo-Saxons themselves had first come to England as raiders, preying on a peaceful Romano-British people. Over time, some had stayed and settled, consolidating their hold, especially in eastern regions – which was where the Danish Vikings were in time to stay and settle, too.

Not only had the manner of their coming been much the same: the Anglo-Saxons and the Vikings were ethnically and culturally close. Both were of broadly Germanic origins. Though that word may mislead, as well: when we describe the Anglo-Saxons as Germans we easily forget that their homelands lay in the far northwest of what we now think of as Germany – in many cases, indeed, in modern Denmark. Beowulf, we know, had been born in southern Sweden; Heorot had been built on Danish Zealand.

This is not to say that the Danish Vikings were ethnically identical to the Jutes. They seem to have emerged as a people in Denmark's more easterly islands, a little after the Jutish heyday. It does, however, make it arguable that, all things considered, the Anglo-Saxons were for the most part very nearly as Scandinavian as the Vikings.

Their religious beliefs were broadly similar to the Vikings', too. They called Woden 'Odin', Frigg 'Freya' and Thunor 'Thor', but these are all recognizably the same deities, and there were clear resemblances in everything from shipbuilding techniques to

Влѣ ѕ҃. у҃. аі. Игореви же възрастъшю. и хожаше
по Олзѣ и слоушашае. и приведоша емоу женоу ѿ Пль-
скова. именемъ Ѡлгоу. Влѣ ѕ҃ у҃ ві. Влѣ ѕ҃ у҃ гі.
Влѣ ѕ҃ у҃ ді. Влѣ ѕ҃ у҃ еі. Иде Олегъ на Грекы. и
Гора ѡставивъ Кїевѣ. поя множество варягъ. и сло
венъ. и чюдь. и словене. и кривичи. и мерю. и деревля
ны. и радимичи. и поляны. и сѣверо. и вятичи. и хо
рваты. и доулѣбы. и тиверци. яже соуть толко
вины. си вси звахоуть ѿ грекъ Великая Скоуфь. и с сими
со всѣми поиде Ѡлегъ на конех и на кораблех. и бѣ
числомъ кораблей .в҃. прииде къ Црю граду. и греци
замкоша Соудъ. а град затвориша.

И вылѣзе Ѡлегъ на брегъ. и воевати нача. и много оу
бийства сотвори. ѡколо града грекомъ. и разбиша
многы полаты. и пожгоша церкви. а их же имаху
плѣнникы. ѡвѣх посекаху. другыя же му
чаху. иныя же растреляху. а другыя
в море вметаху. и ина многа твораху русь
грекомъ. елико же ратнии творять.

weaponry and from poetry to art. This wouldn't normally surprise us. Scandinavia and northern Germany are neighbours. It's just that English convention has framed these cultures so distinctly.

## Geographical imperatives

There were differences, to be sure. In Norway especially, living conditions were that much tougher than they were in the countries to the south. The interior was mostly mountainous, so people clung to the coast, where there were pasture and plots for farming beside long, deep, sheltered inlets or fjords. But space was in short supply, and it was hard for a young man of ambition to establish himself and his family. It's no surprise that the first Viking raids are believed to have set out from there.

Sweden and Denmark were more forgiving, with kinder conditions and more fertile land to go around. Even so, things weren't easy. People were thrown together, often in communal longhouses where the chieftain and his relations lived cheek-by-jowl with one another. And with their livestock, whose winter quarters were at one end of the house. Smaller dwellings clustered round this central core.

**BELOW: Norse reenactors form a shield wall during a battle demonstration at the Yorvik festival in York, England.**

## Band of brothers

Behind every longship was a longhouse, indeed: the tradition of living close together with complete loyalty to – and trust in – their community and their chieftain would have stood the Vikings in good stead when they went to sea – and indeed when they went to war.

Vikings were to kill and plunder as far south as Seville; as far east as Constantinople. Raiders from Norway mostly took a more westerly course, stopping off at Orkney and Shetland en route for Ireland with its ancient monasteries.

An occasional adventure to start with, 'going viking' became a way of life. Norsemen established bases at Dublin and on the Seine and Loire in France where they could spend the winter, ready to resume with the return of the raiding season in the spring. Swedish warbands looked south and east, finding their way down the Russian river-system to the Black Sea.

The rewards of the raiding life could be great. But it's unlikely to have been a choice in the first instance. Rather, it became more or less a necessity as generations passed and young men struggled to establish themselves in countries so chronically short of cultivable, settleable land. The same imperative seems to have driven the Vikings' westward expansion across the Atlantic – to Iceland, Greenland and, finally, North America.

**THE REWARDS OF THE RAIDING LIFE COULD BE GREAT.**

Astonishing achievements. At bottom, though, the Viking way of life doesn't seem to have been so very different from that of the Anglo-Saxons, a few centuries earlier.

## A history in England

The Anglo-Saxons had come a long way since then, however. They had been in England long enough to have a history in the country. By the time the Vikings landed at Lindisfarne, the landing of Hengist and Horsa in England lay approximately 340 years in the past. A bigger gap, in other words, than that between Britain's Act of Union (1707) and the present day.

Much had happened in that time, though broadly speaking we can see a progression towards the concentration of power in fewer but larger kingdoms. Mercia had come to prominence under Penda (655; r. c. 625–55) and Wulfhere (675; r. 658–75), though

**ABOVE: It may not be much to look at now, but Offa's Dyke was an important defensive fortification – and a major statement on the part of the Mercian king.**

succession struggles went on for generations. At various points, it pitched into civil war. In 757, King Aethelbald (r. 716–570) was assassinated by his bodyguards, apparently on behalf of a certain Beornred, of whom nothing else is known. Within weeks he was toppled by Offa (r. 757–96).

He's most famous now for his 'dyke' – a defensive earthwork a little over 130km (82 miles) in length running down the border between Mercia and Wales. (The name 'Mercia' literally meant 'the people of the boundary' – indeed, this area is known as the 'Welsh Marches' to this day.) But this was only part of an ambitious programme of kingdom-building on Offa's part. Not only did he consolidate his hold over Mercia and, with it, much of the English Midlands, he established his overlordship of Sussex and even Kent. This expansion of his influence southwards came at the expense of Wessex, whose King Cynewulf (786; r. 757–86) he defeated at the Battle of Bensington (maybe Benson, Oxfordshire) in 779. Seven years later, Cynewulf was murdered by a political rival, and although Offa isn't suspected of any involvement, he may well have seized the opportunity to put his own man Beorhtric (802; r. 786–802), subsequently his son-in-law, on the Wessex throne.

A rival to Beorhtric's kingship in Wessex, till Offa forced him into Frankish exile, Egbert (c. 775–839; r. 802–9) came back on Beorhtric's death to take the throne. Under his rule, Wessex rebounded. Not only did it succeed in resisting Mercian domination but, in 825, Egbert led his army to a resounding victory over that of Beornwulf of Mercia (826; r. 823–6) at the Battle of Ellendun, near present-d

Mercia's ascendancy rapidly unravelled. Not only was the way opened for Wessex to take over Kent and Essex but the East Anglians were emboldened to ally themselves with Wessex to bring Mercian domination of their kingdom to an end.

**BELOW: Cynewulf's murder may not have been committed on Offa's orders, but the Mercian king was to be a major beneficiary.**

## Civilization vs savagery

All this history hadn't just been 'water under the bridge' in the most vague and abstract sense. The Anglo-Saxons had been changed by their experiences. They weren't the same reckless raiders who had disembarked in Kent in the fifth century. From their point of view, then, the Vikings did seem very different. They were very

different, indeed. For one thing, the Anglo-Saxons themselves were fairly thoroughly Christianized now. This alone would have been enough to prompt the formation of a new identity.

First, because it gave them common cause with each other, across the kingdoms of the heptarchy, in pursuing a new set of values in their new country. Second, because it set a gulf between this 'new country' and the old one, which had come to seem spiritually and culturally remote. They may have felt a real romantic nostalgia for the warrior life they'd left behind, but they were certain that they had left it behind. If they did see anything of themselves in the Viking raiders, it would have been a warning of what they had been once and might yet be again were they to forsake the path of piety and order.

**OPPOSITE: Egbert's statue at Lichfield Cathedral invests him with an aura of majesty befitting the king who led Wessex to supremacy in southern England.**

For them, the anarchy was over. They were no longer scrabbling in the soil just to get by, but had established prosperous farms and smallholdings. To some extent, they were even urbanized. Things had settled down since the wars of the occupation-era and a steady (if unspectacular) trade in luxury goods had opened up with the continent – with the Kingdom of the Franks and the Low Countries as well as with the 'old country', in northwestern Germany.

'Wics' or trading settlements were springing up at key coastal inlets or riverside sites. Though absolutely minuscule by modern standards, places like Gippeswyc (Ipswich) and Nordwic (Norwich) were well on their way to becoming little towns.

**LEFT: The reconstructed village of West Stow in Suffolk recreates typical living conditions for the majority of the population in Anglo-Saxon England.**

**OPPOSITE: The outside letter 'B' of 'Britain' gets Bede's *Ecclesiastical History*. Off to an appropriately august start in this beautifully illuminated edition.**

Though Romano-British Londinium had been abandoned, an Anglo-Saxon settlement named Lundenwic had sprung up a little way beyond its walls. It belonged to the kingdom of Essex and wasn't very significant. Winchester, by contrast, doesn't seem to have changed much after its abandonment by the Romans. It went on being an important centre as the capital of Wessex.

## Monastic momentum

Despite these developments, in England as elsewhere in Europe at this time, the monasteries were leading society at large. Bede's *Ecclesiastical History of the English People* is oddly titled from a modern point of view: either it's a history of the English people or a history of their church. The reality is, though, that in an age in which other institutions of society and state had yet to take form in any really meaningful sense, the church was the most important driving force.

And not just spiritually: the 'rule' of monastic life laid down by St Benedict of Nursia (c. 480–c. 547) specified that, along with daily services, private prayer and study hours, time had to be set aside for physical labour to mortify the flesh and promote humility of the soul. Monks worked the land, grew fruit, reared livestock, farmed fish, kept bees and promoted pioneering processes in everything from brewing to leather-preparation and textile-manufacture, making monasteries into powerful economic engines.

**THE CHURCH WAS THE MOST IMPORTANT DRIVING FORCE.**

## By the book

They contributed culturally, as well: rich as they were, they played an important part as patrons of the arts and, especially, of learning. With the advent of printing still some centuries off, every book had to be hand-written. That inevitably made them prestige items. Which in turn meant that immense attention was paid to their presentation. They were decoratively illustrated – or 'illuminated' – with exquisite artistry. It mattered both that the redeeming 'Word' of Christ should appear in an appropriately august and splendid style and that the wealth and culture of the monastery that owned the book should be proclaimed. Not that books were ever simply artefacts. Their content clearly mattered.

inter septentrionem et occidentem
locata est · germaniae · galliae ·
hispaniae · maximis europae
partibus ·
multo interuallo aduersa · quae
per milia passuum · dccc · inbore
am longa · latitudinis habet milia
cc · exceptis dumtaxat prolixio
ribus diuersorum promontorio
rum tractibus ·
quibus efficitur ut circuitus eius
quadragies octies · lxxv · milia con
pleat · habet a meridie galliam
belgicam · cuius proximum litus
transmeantibus aperit ciuitas quae
dicitur rutubi portus ·
a gente anglorum nunc corrupte
reptacaestir uocata ·
interposito mari a gessoriaco
morinorum gentis litore proximo ·
traiectu milium L siue ut quidam scripsere stadi
orum · ccccl ·
a tergo autem unde oceano infinito
patet · orcadas insulas habet ·
opima frugibus atque arboribus
insula · et alendis apta pecoribus

VENITE
EX-

Monastic scribes were always going to specialize in religious themes. Hence the biblical allusions in *Beowulf*, but hence too the important body of scriptural commentary written at this time, and the rich literature of hagiography (saints' lives). These placed an emphasis on the miracles performed by the saints themselves or associated with their shrines after they'd been buried. Though nominally factual, they're now generally regarded as being akin to myth.

**OPPOSITE: St Benedict of Nursia was not just a holy man. The monastic rule he introduced was important in establishing the foundations for economic development across much of Europe.**

## A surplus of saints

This period in Anglo-Saxon England has been described as the 'age of saints': every religious foundation and every important family had to have one, it sometimes seems. In Mercia, for example, a devotion arose to Wigstan (c. 849), a royal prince who, however, declined the throne on his father's death, preferring to live a religious life. When he was murdered by an angry courtier, a column of light shot up to heaven from the ground where he had fallen. It remained there, shining brightly, for 30 days, we are told.

Or there's Guthlac of Crowland (674–714), who lived as a hermit on what was then an island in the Fens of Lincolnshire. He is said to have been visited there by demons determined to frighten him out of his faith. 'They were', says Felix, the East Anglian monk who wrote his hagiography:

*ferocious in appearance, terrible in shape with great heads, long necks, thin faces, yellow complexions, filthy beards, shaggy ears, wild foreheads, fierce eyes, foul mouths, horses' teeth, throats vomiting flames, twisted jaws, thick lips, strident voices, singed hair, fat cheeks, pigeons' breasts, scabby thighs, knotty knees, crooked legs, swollen ankles, splay feet, spreading mouths, raucous cries … They grew so terrible to hear with their mighty shriekings that they filled almost the whole intervening space between earth and heaven with their discordant bellowing.*

Guthlac had kinder company in his last days, being overheard chatting amiably with angels who, when the moment came, wafted him heavenwards amid a nectar-like aroma and a beam of light.

## Saintly sisters

St Aethelthryth (c. 636–79) is believed to have been born at Exning, near Newmarket in Suffolk, the daughter of King Anna of East Anglia (c. 654). Her sister Aethelburh (664) was a saint as well – she became Abbess of France's Faremoutiers Abbey. So too was their sister Seaxburh (699).

Their illegitimate half-sister, Wihtburh (743) was to prove no less worthy. She founded a monastery at Dereham, Norfolk. As her supporters toiled to build it, the story goes, they grew hungry and thirsty and were reaching the point of collapse when the Virgin Mary sent a pair of female deer to provide them all with milk.

Aethelthryth, who had resolved from childhood to remain a virgin, persuaded two successive husbands to respect this vow. When the second, King Ecgfrith of Northumbria (c. 645–85), thought better of this agreement, Aethelthryth was forced to flee and to take refuge on the Isle of Ely. Now only nominally an island, Ely, in northern Cambridgeshire, was at this time truly surrounded by the open waters of the Fens.

Aethelthryth died, her virginity intact, and was laid to rest in a white marble tomb. When her sister Seaxburh had it opened 16 years later so Aethelthryth's corpse could be placed in Ely's new abbey church (later its cathedral), her body was found to have remained completely uncorrupted.

## Of darkness and Danes

The conventional designation of the period from the fall of Rome to the tenth century as the 'Dark Ages' has been coming under mounting criticism from historians for some time now. Anglo-Saxon England certainly seems to have been clambering up into the light – at least until the onset of the Viking Age. There's no doubt that the tumult that this brought placed all this peaceful development in jeopardy, and cast a long, dark, Danish shadow across the land.

The underachievers of the Viking group, the Danes didn't discover America as the Norsemen did, nor found Kiev or sail to Byzantium like the Swedes, but they had a decisive impact on English history. By the ninth century, they were practically commuting across the North Sea. And coming in greater and greater strength, smaller warbands of just a ship or two's strength massing into major fleets with thousands of warriors – like the 'Great Heathen Army' the *Anglo-Saxon Chronicle* reported having landed on England's eastern coast in 865 to begin a 14-year campaign – not just of raiding but to some extent of conquest, too.

This force, though predominantly Danish, included Norwegians and Swedes as well. The plan appears to have been to attack the kingdoms of Northumbria, East Anglia, Mercia and Wessex – which by this time meant pretty much the whole of England.

One distinguished casualty of the conflict was King Edmund of East Anglia (869; r. c. 855–69). By all accounts, he was 'wise and venerable … meek and humble in his ways'. He was pious; tough with oppressors but generous to the poor.

ABOVE: A representation of St Etheldreda in a stained glass window in the church consecrated to her in Ely.

## History meets hagiography

A more prosaic, conventional historiography has concluded that he died in battle, leading his forces against the Great Heathen Army. But his *Life*, written by Aelfric of Eynsham (c. 955–c. 1010), has him refusing to fight, mindful of Christ's injunction to St Peter not to defend him when the 'cruel Jews' came to arrest him in the Garden of Gethsemane but to lay down his sword.

The king was duly captured by the Danish leader, Hinguar, a savage 'wolf', who mocked and insulted Edmund and demanded that he forswear his faith. When he refused, they thrashed him with switches (thin, flexible shoots from a tree) then tied him to a tree and shot arrows at him until, in Aelfric's memorable description, the shafts stuck out of his body like a hedgehog's spines.

As Edmund slumped there, dying, calling out to Christ, Hinguar finished him off in the most demeaning way by chopping off his head at a single stroke. To complete his degradation, Hinguar had his men conceal the king's head in a thicket of briars, so his supporters wouldn't be able to find it for burial with the rest of his body.

Neatly balancing out the wolfishness of Hinguar (in token, presumably, of Christianity's civilizing power), a real wolf is said to have come and stood guard over Edmund's severed head, so no scavenging beast would think of marring it before it could be found. Meanwhile, the head kept calling out its whereabouts to the king's searching men. When they finally located it, and set off home with it to lay it in the church, the wolf kept them company until they got to the town gates, at which point he took himself off back into the woods.

## Divine punishment

Edmund was ceremonially lain to rest and, in the years that followed, pilgrims flocked to his shrine. Many brought precious treasures as offerings. One night, a group of eight thieves came and tried to force an entry to his chapel: some took a sledgehammer to the lock; some tried to prise the door open from underneath; one took a ladder to a window to get in that way. Suddenly they were all seized by some sacred force, frozen fast to their various tools, unable to release them or make their escape. They were held that way until staff arrived to open the church next morning, and were tried and hanged.

One Leofstan, a proud and wealthy man who doubted claims that the body of the saint was uncorrupted, after years in his tomb, ordered officials to open it so he could see. Edmund's body was revealed – as fresh as it had been the day of his interment. But Leofstan went mad and died from his distraction.

These preliminary hostilities completed, the Vikings ended up leaving East Anglia alone in return for a supply of horses for their campaign in the rest of the country. Quite how interested the Vikings were in enduring conquest is not clear. To begin with, at least, they seem to have been as interested in operating a 'protection racket' as in taking territory. In return for a massive payment, they agreed to leave Mercia in peace, as well. The king of Wessex bought them off in the same way.

## Enter Alfred

This was a slightly ignominious entrance into the historical record for King Alfred the Great (c. 848–99; r. (Wessex) 871–c.

886; (King of the Anglo-Saxons) c. 886–99), accordingly. The son of Aethelwulf (858; r. 839–58), Alfred had succeeded to his throne only after his elder brothers, Aethelbald (860; r. 858–60), Aethelbert (866; r. 860–6) and Aethelred I (c. 845–871; r. 865–81) had reigned in Wessex. A still older brother, Aethelstan (852; r. 839–51), had ruled under their father's overlordship in Kent. In that capacity, he'd won what has gone down in history as England's earliest naval victory – against a Viking fleet off Sandwich.

Alfred, however, found within a few weeks that the peace he'd bought might only be very temporary. The Great Heathen Army now re-invaded Mercia and took the kingdom before turning once more to Wessex, where it won a succession of victories. Alfred clung on, though, and the Danes directed their attentions to the other Anglo-Saxon kingdoms, where they made further conquests over the next few years. By 878, Wessex stood alone. Nor did it stand very securely, Alfred being forced to flee for the safety of the Somerset Levels – a wetland area in the southwest of England.

There, the story goes, he lay low in the cottage of a poor old woman who had no idea that she was hosting her incognito king. One day, when she had to go out for a while, she left a batch of cakes cooking by the fire, asking her guest to take them off when they were done. Alfred, absorbed by the responsibilities of office and the stress of war, forgot her orders and allowed the cakes to burn. When his hostess returned, she gave him a fearful dressing-down. That appears to have been Alfred's lowest point.

**BELOW: Vikings belabour King Edmund as they drive him from his throne in an illuminated *Life of Edmund* (c. 1130).**

**THE KINGDOM OF 'ENGLAND' WAS DOGGED BY DIVISION AT THE TOP.**

He emerged from his hideaway to lead his army to victory against the Vikings on Salisbury Plain at the Battle of Edington. The Danes under Guthrum (c. 865–90) were forced into retreat. They were cornered and, a fortnight later, compelled to surrender, Guthrum agreeing to convert to Christianity.

Not only did King Alfred baptize him personally: he ceremonially adopted the Viking as his son. The treaty they signed allowed Guthrum and the Danes to occupy territories in the north and east of England; as long as they stayed out of Wessex, all could live in peace. This principle established, it was hardened in 886 into an agreement that the Vikings would have self-rule in their own separate realm, the 'Danelaw'. Alfred, meanwhile, made himself 'King of the Anglo-Saxons'.

## Down with the Danelaw

His son Edward the Elder (c. 874–924; r. 899–924) succeeded him – though not without opposition from the son of Aethelred I. Things were still feeling fairly provisional in England. An army from the Danelaw pushed south into Wessex in 910, but was emphatically repulsed, and after this things started to seem more stable. His son and successor Aethelstan (c. 894–939; r. 924–39) consolidated his hold on all the southern kingdoms and made conquering inroads deep into the Danelaw. In 928, Aethelstan became the first ruler to call himself 'King of the English' – though this was as yet more aspiration than established fact.

The Battle of Brunanburh (937) was a real engagement that quickly took on mythic status. It is widely believed to have been fought at Bromborough, south of Birkenhead on the Wirral Peninsula. Pitching Aethelstan's forces against those of the Danelaw, the Scots and an assortment of Viking and Gaelic warlords from the Scottish Isles and Ireland, it was commemorated in a famous Anglo-Saxon poem.

*Never, before this, were more men in this island slain by the sword's edge – as books and aged sages confirm – since Angles and Saxons sailed here …*

ABOVE: **Some scholars see the Battle of Brunanburh (937) as the start of English history.**

Aethelstan's victory wasn't complete – he'd hoped to unite the whole of Britain under 'English' rule – but it left Wessex strong, and the Danelaw living on borrowed time. Its Norwegian ruler Eric Bloodaxe (954; r. c. 947–8; 952–4) was forced out by Edward's son Eadred (923–55; r. 946–55).

Despite its new security, the kingdom of 'England' was dogged by division at the top. The lamentable (if quite possibly legendary) end of King Edward the Martyr (c. 962–78; r. 975–8) is a case in point. He is said to have been assassinated by retainers of his half-brother – and of course successor – Aethelred (r. 978–1016). 'No worse deed for the English race was done than this was,' the anonymous monk who wrote the *Peterborough Chronicle* opined:

*…since they first sought out the land of Britain. Men murdered him, but God exalted him. In life he was an earthly king; after death he is now a heavenly saint.*

Quite what was so saintly about him isn't clear. The development of a cult of martyrdom around his relics seems to have been encouraged by Aethelred's enemies to embarrass him. It spread far and wide, though – and (oddly, it might be thought) has been enduringly important for the Orthodox churches of Eastern Europe.

OPPOSITE: **Alfred the Great, king first of Wessex and then of the Anglo-Saxons, both conquered and Christianized the invading Danes.**

**RIGHT: A stone in Corfe Castle, Dorset, commemorates the millennium of the death of King Edward the Martyr in 978. Men murdered him, but God exalted him,' the *Peterborough Chronicle* said of Edward. His half-brother Aethelred seems to have had him killed so he could claim his throne.**

## Ill-advised?

Aethelred's reign was, notoriously, to be unhappy. He's gone down in tradition as 'Aethelred the Unready', though the Anglo-Saxon word *unraed* is probably better translated as 'ill-advised'.

He undoubtedly found himself in difficult circumstances. Aethelstan may have put the Danelaw in its place but Scandinavian Vikings were still raiding regularly, sometimes on an awe-inspiring scale. In 991, the *Anglo-Saxon Chronicle* reports, a fleet of over 90 longships appeared off Folkestone, Kent. It landed an army of up to 3000 men – including both Norwegian and Danish Vikings. Marching up to Maldon, in Essex, it defeated an Anglo-Saxon force there but withdrew on the payment of a gigantic ransom. Not just that, but a ransom that had to be renewed each year; Aethelred had to levy a special tax on his subjects, the 'Danegeld', so the payment could be met. Popular historiography has it that agreeing to this was not just weak on Aethelred's part but self-evidently stupid, though it's hard to see what real alternative he had.

One mistake he certainly could have avoided was ordering the St Brice's Day Massacre in 1002. Danes living in English territories (mostly serving as bodyguards to English nobles) were summarily put to death. We've no real idea how many were murdered in this way, but it was conspicuously counterproductive, triggering a spate of punitive actions by Sweyn Forkbeard, King of Denmark and Norway (c. 960–1014; r. 986–1014). These only crescendoed as the years went on, Sweyn having sensed his opportunity to build on earlier successes. By 1013, Aethelred had been forced into exile in Normandy and Anglo-Saxon England had a Danish king.

Only briefly, however – for the following year Sweyn Forkbeard died and Aethelred was able to retake his throne. But his own son Edmund Ironside (c. 960–1016: r. April–November 1016) was soon dead – quite possibly assassinated (stabbed numerous times while seated on his privy, according to some reports).

Sweyn's son Cnut the Great (1035; r. 1016–35) took England's throne, uniting this realm with those he'd inherited from his father in Denmark and Norway and consequently creating a sort of Viking empire with the North Sea at its centre.

## Ruling the Waves?

It is to the twelfth-century chronicler Henry of Huntingdon (c. 1088–1157) that we owe the story of King Canute and his confrontation with the waves. He recorded it as an example of Cnut's profound humility and wisdom.

Wearying of the flattery of courtiers who told him he was so powerful that the very elements would do his bidding, he had them take his throne and set it up in the shallows of the sea as the tide advanced. This done, he took his seat, attended by his retainers, and, as the waters lapped around his feet, sternly commanded the waves to desist. On no account must they wet his feet or dampen his royal robe, he said.

The sea, of course, took absolutely no notice. Cnut warned his assembled courtiers to temper their praises in the future, for only Heaven had authority over the natural world.

It is in the nature of myth that a story's accepted meaning may change from age to age. In modern usage, it has as often as not been assumed that Cnut actually expected the waves to do his bidding, being guilty of extravagantly overweening pride.

# ARTHURIAN LEGEND

All medieval Europe loved the chivalrous ideal exemplified by King Arthur and his knights. To this day, their stories are enjoyed around the world.

The Battle of Mount Badon hadn't been important only because it represented a rare reverse for the Anglo-Saxon incomers. It mattered more because the British force was said to have been led by a certain Arthur Pendragon, or King Arthur. The *Historia Brittonum*'s account of his contribution is tantalizing, offering no specific details to speak of but high-flown praise: 'Nine hundred fell by his hand alone,' it assures us. Hardly an inauspicious start for one of England's most illustrious mythic heroes, then, but an underwhelming one, given the importance he would one day have.

Geoffrey of Monmouth takes up the narrative. His King Arthur is a more rounded, complex figure – though still not the romantic one we may think of today.

**OPPOSITE: King Arthur claims his crown, as imagined by Charles Ernest Butler (1864–1933). Arthurian legend took on a whole new lease of life in modern times.**

## Magical Merlin

Geoffrey definitely adds value, though. Not only does he give us a more rounded, lifelike Arthur by coming up with a father, Uther Pendragon, for him, but he gives him an attendant magician too. Merlin is believed to have been a composite of the mythic Welsh sorcerer Myrddin Wellt and the Romano-British hero Ambrosius Aurelianus, another doughty fighter against the Saxons.

The supernatural dimension undoubtedly gives us a much more intriguing story. Geoffrey's Merlin was begotten on a mortal woman by a fairy incubus, who stole into her bed and seduced her, we are told. But we're not told who this woman was. She was a princess, it's tantalizingly suggested, but we're never given her name – still less any information on her life and background. Geoffrey strikes us as incurious. Generally, he isn't as concerned with what we would call psychology as later writers of Arthurian romances were to some extent. This may help give his tales a gutsy energy but it also leaves them lacking a degree of deeper imaginative interest.

**THE SUPERNATURAL DIMENSION GIVES US A MUCH MORE INTRIGUING STORY.**

Merlin grows up to serve Uther Pendragon, magically giving him the appearance of his arch-enemy Gorlois of Tintagel, Duke of Cornwall, so he can sleep with his wife Igraine, and it's thus that the young Prince Arthur is conceived. In later versions of the story, Gorlois dies and Uther marries Igraine before the boy is born so that he can be as it were retroactively legitimized. Not in Geoffrey's story, though. Arthur's 'respectability' in this ultra-proper sense doesn't seem to be of too much interest to him. Which, once again, may strike the twenty-first-century reader as refreshing, though it goes along with an unceremonious attitude to individual characters, their experiences and their feelings, that can leave them feeling two-dimensional from a modern point of view.

## Conquest and calm

Back in the real world, meanwhile, English history had been anything but romantic. The only actual resemblance between the world of King Arthur and that of the English eleventh and twelfth centuries was that both worlds featured Saxons being slaughtered.

ABOVE: **Merlin's mother – a mortal woman – was seduced by a fairy incubus, displayed in this fifteenth-century illustration, the Maître d'Adelaide de Savoie, in diabolic terms.**

Anglo-Saxon England had of course been brought to a violent end by the Norman Conquest (1066). The descendants of Norwegian Vikings, the Normans had been much changed by several generations of settlement in northern France. Some might say they had been civilized, though they'd lost nothing of their old aggression or fighting skill.

Conventional English historiography has tended to see the whole conflict decided by the Battle of Hastings – and it's

**RIGHT: After his victory at Hastings, William's coronation may have seemed conclusive, but the 'Norman Conquest' had arguably only just begun.**

true that the Normans' victory there had brought William I, 'the Conqueror' (c. 1028–87; r. 1066–87), London and the English throne. Much of the kingdom had continued to resist, however. The Harrying of the North (1069–70) that William undertook to put down resistance there had involved all but genocidal levels of repression.

Cruel as it was, it successfully quelled the worst of the opposition to Norman rule, and England was pacified – if not perhaps at real peace. William's famous Domesday Book was his way of essentially inventorying the contents of his new kingdom as a preliminary to handing its wealth and resources over to be managed by his hand-picked Norman lords.

As time went on, Anglo-Norman England would be torn on the one hand by violent succession struggles within the ruling elite and on the other by cycles of rebellion and repression (after the North it would be the turn of Wales). But there were also to be protracted periods of calm.

Life went back to something like normal. The monasteries, to some extent protected from the turbulence, picked up the cultural reins. It was of course at this time that Geoffrey of Monmouth wrote his *History of the Kings*. He dedicated it to Robert, Earl of Gloucester (c. 1090–1147), the illegitimate son of Henry I (c. 1068–1135). Henry's court was hardly Camelot, nor he King Arthur.

Not least because there were real suspicions that he'd had his predecessor William Rufus (c. 1056–1100; r. 1087–1100) killed (he'd been hit by a stray arrow while out hunting in the New Forest). Even so, his reign had brought a degree of stability to England.

**BELOW: The Domesday Book brought all to order, it appeared, effectively inventorying England. But resistance to the Normans was to continue for years.**

ABOVE: 'How Mordred was slain by Arthur, and how by him Arthur was wounded to the death.' Arthur Rackham (1867–1939) captures both the horror and the romance of Arthurian legend.

## Freedom fighter

The general consensus has been, however, that the Normans are the Saxons in Geoffrey's story – another alien occupier to be sent packing by a Celtic king. In wishful thinking if not in real history. Though his version of events does involve a fair amount of fantasy and enchantment, the Arthur he describes is a man of action; a freedom fighter – even an empire-builder.

Briefly, we're told that Arthur fought a series of battles with the Saxons. He won his final victory at Badon Hill. Having secured his authority in England, he went on to put down the Picts and Scots, then to extend his dominion over Orkney and Ireland. And even Iceland, Norway, Denmark and Gaul (France). In the meantime, he had married, Geoffrey of Monmouth tells us, but while he'd been campaigning on the continent his wife Guinevere had become involved with his nephew Mordred.

Not only had this traitor taken advantage of his uncle's absence to have an affair with his wife, he'd mounted a rebellion against the king and usurped his throne. When Arthur was back in Britain, they had met in battle at Camlann and Arthur killed him, but the dying Mordred had given Arthur his own death-wound.

### A tale of two Arthurs

Stirring stuff, but – notwithstanding the element of enchantment – very much a straightforward adventure story. There are two Arthurs when we read the literature overall. The first – whose story we have just read – was a (semi-?) legendary leader of the late-fifth and early-sixth centuries who led the defence of Britain against its Saxon invaders. Most of the stories that made it into the mythic legacy aren't about this ruler or his epic combat, though. Rather, they centre on a second King Arthur who, in high-medieval times, held court at Camelot – a place of the utmost chivalry and honour – surrounded by his Knights of the Round Table.

## From Arimathea to Avalon

What was believed to be Arthur and Guinevere's grave was found by monks at Somerset's Glastonbury Abbey in the twelfth century, close to the Lake of Avalon. More than this, though, Glastonbury has for many centuries had a special place where pagan meets Christian myth, for it was reputedly here that Joseph of Arimathea came in the aftermath of Jesus's death and resurrection.

No one actually knows where Arimathea is, but its most famous son was the Joseph who in the Gospels (Matthew 27, 57, for example) went to the authorities after Christ's death on the cross and gained their permission to give the body a fitting burial. Joseph placed it in the tomb he'd bought in preparation for his own end.

This is where Joseph leaves the scriptural account, but he was to take on a life of his own in the apocryphal literature in the centuries that followed. Writers agreed that, after Christ had left the world behind to ascend to heaven, Joseph had set out journeying, with relics of his Saviour. The most famous of these was the so-called Holy Grail.

Depending on which author you read, this was either the dish the lamb had rested in when Christ and his Apostles ate their Last Supper together or the chalice from which they'd shared the wine. (The same cup, some said, was to be held up beside Christ's beaten, tattered body at the Crucifixion to catch the blood that came streaming down from its pierced side.) Whatever it was, the Grail became an object of chivalric quest in its own right.

Legend had it that Joseph's wanderings eventually brought him to Somerset. Laying down on the ground to sleep, he stuck his staff upright in the ground. Overnight, it took root and burst into leaf as the Glastonbury Thorn. Despite the specifically Christian associations of this myth, Glastonbury has become an important site for neo-pagans in the modern age.

The temptation is to assume that, given the comparative simplicity with which his story is told, the first King Arthur is historical in a way the second one isn't. But we've really no basis for that belief at all. Geoffrey's tale is just a different kind of fantasy. The second King Arthur was to take shape only gradually and cumulatively in the romances of a range of writers and poets over the remaining centuries of the Middle Ages. But one man in particular did more to 'launch' him than any other, establishing the values he stood for and the way he would be seen.

## Morgan le Fay

King Arthur's Camelot offered a rich and varied cast of characters, whom successive writers shaped – and sometimes supplemented – in their own ways. Frequently with very little care for consistency across the different stories. That of Morgan le Fay is a case in point.

'Fay' here just means 'fairy', and in the earliest accounts Morgan seems essentially benign: a protector for King Arthur – something like the fairy godmother of later tales. Her magic powers are very much those of a healer, and a bringer of spiritual resolution. It was to her at Avalon that Arthur, mortally wounded at the Battle of Camlann, was borne by boat to receive the best in comfort and in care.

Despite this more maternal side, she's rather more like Arthur's enchanted sister (or half-sister: she's the daughter of Igraine and Gorlois in Geoffrey of Monmouth's *Life of Merlin* (1148)). She can show jealousy – bitterly resenting Guinevere, in some accounts. As is often the way with female figures in mythology, admiration of her self-confidence and strength can easily slip over into the perception that she's wayward, wild – and ultimately destructive. She's seen as sexually predatory in her affairs with some of Arthur's knights. By the time we get to Sir Thomas Malory's account, Morgan is malevolence personified, the cause of just about all that's evil in Arthur's world.

### Chrétien at court

Chrétien de Troyes (c. 1135–c. 1185) appears to have been a distinguished poet already when, in 1160, he came to live and work at the court of Marie of France (1145–98), Countess of Champagne. She was the daughter of Eleanor of Aquitaine (1122–1204) and Louis VII of France (1120–80; r. 1137–80). That marriage having produced no male heir, it had been annulled in 1152 and Eleanor had immediately married England's Henry II (1133–89; r. 1154–89).

William the Conqueror's successors had still not given up their title as Dukes of Normandy, so Henry had a strong interest in France. It's believed that the arrival of the royal couple prompted a vogue for the 'Matter of Britain' (see 'Other Matters' box below) in France. It clearly caught Chrétien's imagination. Catering as he largely was to an

**OPPOSITE: Morgan le Fay is brought to thrilling life by Frederick Sandys (1829–1904). Part of the appeal of the Arthurian romances for a buttoned-up Victorian era was the hint of wild eroticism they suggested.**

**THEY UPHOLD THE VALUES NOT JUST OF COURAGE BUT OF CHASTITY.**

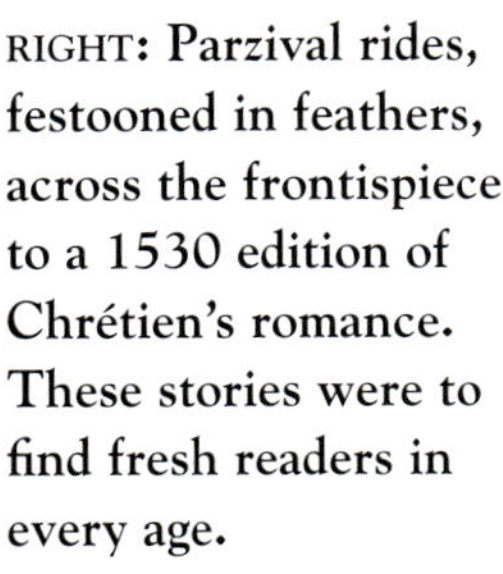

**RIGHT: Parzival rides, festooned in feathers, across the frontispiece to a 1530 edition of Chrétien's romance. These stories were to find fresh readers in every age.**

audience of ladies, he effectively reinvented the Arthurian myths as romances – elegant, poetic and genteel. Knights-errant embark on heroic quests, slaying dragons and saving damsels in distress.

Mostly they're motivated by the desire to demonstrate their devotion to a fair (and generally unyielding) lady. Either way, with notable exceptions, they uphold the values not just of courage but of chastity. Sexual restraint is regarded as a sign of strength.

Chrétien also saw that the chivalric quest could be either allegorically or more directly spiritual, giving the Arthurian material a resonance that (though himself a monk) Geoffrey of Monmouth could never have imagined.

## A romantic weave

Obviously, some things were lost – not least the slightest pretence of real historicity, sketchy as this had been in Geoffrey's work. Neither Chrétien nor the growing school of courtly writers who followed him interested themselves in Arthur's conduct as a real king. For them he was important, first, as a romantic protagonist in his own right and, second, as the centre of a court around which a range of further romantic narratives might revolve. It's not that their England isn't in its way a 'real' country, but it's real as a setting for a succession of appealing stories.

As time went on, these different writers rang the changes on the basic Arthurian scheme, introducing new adventures and fresh characters as they went. There is, accordingly, no single definitive story: more a tapestry of interwoven threads. The narrative that follows seeks to steer a middle course …

## Born to be king

As a boy, it is widely said, young Arthur was raised in ignorance of his true parentage: he was brought up to believe that he was the son of Sir Ector, who adopted him. He considered Sir Ector's son Sir Kay to be his elder brother. Sir Kay would subsequently be his 'seneschal' – the steward at his court.

When Uther Pendragon died a few years later, he apparently left no heir. No one at the royal court was aware of Arthur's existence, let alone his claim to the crown. An angry controversy arose over Uther's succession. It seems to be to Robert de Boron

### Other Matters

Stories of King Arthur and his court were not just set down by English storytellers like Thomas Malory (1415–71). As we have seen, indeed, the Arthurian genre seems to have been started by writers at continental courts. Not just Chrétien de Troyes but Robert de Boron (twelfth–thirteenth centuries), Gottfried von Strassburg (c. 1210), Wolfram von Eschenbach (c. 1160–c. 1220) and a scattering of anonymous poets.

All wrote Arthurian works with British settings, giving more or less weight to their own favoured characters or themes but all taking place in the same courtly context and all committed to the same chivalric code. What was known as the 'Matter of Britain' was available as a sort of ready-made romantic realm. Rich in narratives of love and adventure, it could be shaped by each writer individually to suit his own expressive instincts – rather as the western genre was to become in modern times.

There were other acknowledged story-cycles. The Matter of France (or, rather, of the Franks, as we'd see it now) offered stories of Charlemagne's Empire – so the recent past. The Matter of Rome did not just treat of Rome but of classical antiquity more generally. It included stories of the Trojan War and the rise of Alexander the Great (356–23 BCE; r. 336–23 BCE).

**ABOVE: In Malory's *Morte d'Arthur*, Merlin is given the infant Arthur and brings him up. Here we see him accepting his charge, in a work by Austrian painter Emil Johann Lauffer (1837–1909).**

that we owe the story of the sword in the stone, which shows Arthur stumbling into his royal status as if by chance. A boulder abruptly appeared in a churchyard (in some versions with a heavy iron anvil on top of it); standing, thrust deep into it, was an ornate sword.

Whoever could draw it out, an inscription round its hilt asserted, would be the rightful king of Britain. Young heroes came from every corner of the country to make their claim. But all in vain – strong and resolute though the pretenders invariably were, the sword stood obdurately firm, completely stuck.

The 15-year-old Prince Arthur came into town, however, serving the young Sir Kay as his knightly attendant or squire. He slipped up by forgetting to bring his master's sword. In a panic, he went off to look for a replacement weapon, and saw this one sticking out of its stone in the local churchyard. Walking over to it, he gave the hasp a tug, whereupon it slipped out smoothly and he ran off relieved to give it to Sir Kay. Only then was the inscription noticed. Young Arthur had to explain where he'd round the sword. No one understood how he had been able to prise it free. But, by way of demonstration, Arthur slid it back into the stone and out again without the slightest effort – a mark, it was clear, of his regal destiny.

## Defence of the realm

As England's teenage king, Arthur had to deal with a rebellion by 11 local rulers. He gathered his knights around him and went to war. The strongest and bravest young noblemen flocked to Camelot to join him and to fight alongside him against the foe.

It was at around this time that Arthur married Guinevere, and it was her father, King Leodegrance of Cameliard (possibly Cornwall) who gave him a great round table as a wedding gift. Arthur set it up at the centre of his court at Camelot. Its great beauty, as far as he was concerned, was that he could sit around it with his knights, and none of them would have any special precedence over the rest.

ABOVE: **Gottfried von Strassburg, who wrote one of the most famous versions of the Tristan legend, appears here in a woodcut of 1880.**

## A second sword

With his gallant knights beside him and with Merlin as his constant counsellor, Arthur won all these early wars. But he was also immeasurably assisted by the power of his enchanted sword, which was known as Excalibur. In some versions of the story, this was the sword he had drawn from the stone as a 15-year-old. In other accounts, that sword either doesn't feature at all or is lost or broken. Arthur was left weaponless and had to turn to Merlin for advice.

It was on the magician's instructions that he went to the lake at Avalon, sometimes identified with Glastonbury in Somerset. (As King Alfred had found, that part of southwest England was under water in medieval times. Present-day Glastonbury Tor was actually an island.) Tied up by a bank, he found a little boat. Prompted by Merlin, he set off out into the middle of the lake.

RIGHT: This round table, of painted oak, hangs in the Great Hall of Winchester Castle. Made as late as 1275, it has no conceivable claim to authenticity.

**RIGHT: Arthur is told about the sword Excalibur by the Lady of the Lake.**

Suddenly, a beautiful lady arose from the quiet waters: it was she who handed him the sword Excalibur.

Unsurprisingly, the different medieval writers disagree on the identity of this Lady of the Lake. But several see her as the enchantress Viviane. For some early writers she appears to have been a sort of female alter-ego for Merlin; more often, though, she's viewed as the magician's friend or mystic lover.

Excalibur, it is generally agreed, made the man who wielded it invincible in battle. There simply was no fight it would not win. According to some sources, its scabbard had special powers as well, protecting its wearer from sustaining the slightest scratch.

## Sir Lancelot du Lac

The Lady of the Lake has another important role in Arthurian legend. In some sources it is she who brings up Arthur's great friend, Sir Lancelot. The son of King Bann of Benwick and Queen Elaine, he'd been an infant when his family were forced to flee their Gallic kingdom after its invasion by King Claudas, his mother too busy tending his wounded father to look after him. The Lady of the Lake had snatched him and brought him up in her enchanted realm beneath the water. Once he was grown up she took him to King Arthur's court.

He hit it off with the young king and soon became his boon companion. Unfortunately, he hit it off with Guinevere as well. In some versions, theirs was a chaste affair: Lancelot pined away with longing for a love he sublimated into service to his mistress. He travelled far and wide, carrying out heroic exploits in her honour. This Lancelot has been seen by some scholars as a symbol of suppressed male sexual desire: he has bouts of madness, triggered by the attentions of seductive women. In other versions, though – unusually for the chivalric romances – there's no suggestion of suppression: Lancelot and Guinevere become passionately involved.

**EXCALIBUR MADE THE MAN WHO WIELDED IT INVINCIBLE IN BATTLE.**

## An unworthy ride

Lancelot doesn't appear in Geoffrey's *History*. He seems to have been introduced by Chrétien de Troyes (though he may have heard of him from some other mythic source, now lost). In *Lancelot, the Knight of the Cart* (c. 1175), he happened along at Arthur's court just after Queen Guinevere had been abducted by Mealagant (literally 'Evildoer'), the son of King Bagdemagus, lord of the domain of death. Lancelot galloped off with Arthur's trusted friend, Sir Gawain, in pursuit.

So hard did he ride to save the queen that his mount died. Gawain lent him a spare horse, but he rode this one to its death as well. Gawain wasn't able to give him another one. At that point a dwarf came up driving a cart. Guinevere was being held at Maleagant's castle at Gorre, he informed them: he would take them to her if they would only climb aboard. Gawain refused. It was beneath a knight's dignity, he said, to travel in that style. He

le segond

lun

Sire chevalier fait monseigneur
gauvain car ales jus de la char
rette et montes sur ce cheval q̃
moult est bon ançoys que pl⁹
grant honte vous en viengne.
Dehait ait fait le nain qui ce
loera ne il nen fera riens car il ma creante q̃
il venra huy toute iour iusques au vespre sur
ma charette et lancelot luy dist que il nait
ia garde. car il nen descendra huy mais iusq̃s
a donc que ilz seront herbergies. Certes fait

was going to follow along on horseback or not at all. Lancelot didn't like the idea any more than Gawain did, but he had to save Guinevere so swallowed his pride and scrambled up into the cart.

OPPOSITE: Lancelot makes the ultimate sacrifice – riding in a cart for the sake of Guinevere – in this illustration to a fourteenth-century manuscript.

## Quest accomplished

Many adventures awaited them on their journey. The two eventually parted company. Lancelot had to deal with a group of men wielding axes; a hostile army; an assortment of menacing knights and sinister seductresses – as well as genuine damsels in distress. But he kept his purpose and his conduct true and, finally, his persistence was rewarded when he got to Gorre and found Guinevere imprisoned in a tower at Maleagant's castle.

He was nonplussed by her reaction, though. Taken aback by her coldness, her apparent lack of gratitude, he was unsure how to proceed. Guinevere had been offended, she revealed apologetically afterwards, because he had momentarily hesitated to get into the cart, setting his own status above her welfare. Now softened, she allowed him to climb up to the window of her tower, bend back the bars and make his way into her chamber.

LEFT: Lancelot takes on all comers at a tournament – and on Guinevere's orders deliberately loses – in an illustration from a sixteenth-century French edition of Chrétien de Troyes' romance.

There, says Chrétien:

*She stretched out her arms and pulled him close, clutching him tightly to her bosom, guiding him into the bed beside her … Their pleasure was unlimited as they kissed and caressed each other; their joy such as was never heard or known.*

When next day the suspicious Maleagant saw signs of forced entry at the window and denounced Guinevere publicly as an adulteress, Lancelot challenged him to a duel to defend her honour. This fight was postponed for a year after the intervention of Maleagant's father, during which time Lancelot was subjected to further tests. And taken prisoner by a second dwarf. In the meantime, Guinevere was allowed to return home to Camelot (and her husband!).

## Honour and betrayal

**SELF-ABASING OBEDIENCE ON THE PART OF THE KNIGHT WAS VITAL.**

Lancelot managed to trick his second captor into freeing him to fulfil his promise to fight Maleagant. He set off for Gorre in good time for the contracted duel. He was even able to take a detour via Camelot, taking in a tournament there en route. Guinevere asked him to prove his love for her by losing his bouts at jousting.

When he acceded to her wishes, the queen was so delighted that she passed a message to him, allowing him to win his tourneys after all. The tyranny of the lady's whim was to become an important theme of the courtly love tradition: self-abasing obedience on the part of the knight was vital.

Arriving at Gorre, Lancelot presented himself for combat as he'd promised, only to be quietly overpowered and imprisoned by a group of Maleagant's retainers. By the time the day of their duel came, he'd been whisked away to a tower Maleagant had built in preparation. As the time of their encounter approached, with Lancelot nowhere to be seen, it appeared that he had failed to keep his word. Maleagant was only too happy for this assumption to go unchallenged. He went to Camelot to crow before the court that Lancelot had pledged to fight but failed to show. Gawain offered to fight in his stead.

In the event, however, weary and weak, Lancelot was rescued from his imprisonment, helped by Maleagant's sister – who

# PARFIT, GENTIL ...

The medieval ideal of chivalry was to be summed up by the English poet Geoffrey Chaucer in *The Canterbury Tales* (c. 1390). 'A knight ther was, and that a worthy man ... ', he wrote: 'That fro the tyme that he first bigan/To riden out, he loved chivalrie,/Trouthe and honour, fredom [the word here means 'nobility'] and curtesye.'

Knights were first and foremost soldiers – in this they were much like the warrior elite who had surrounded Beowulf and other ancient chieftains. They spent their days drilling in sword- and shield-play, then, and in horsemanship. (Riding was an important mark of social rank – hence the French word chevalier – 'horseman' – for the English 'knight'.) There were special skills involved in fighting on horseback, so typically the knight spent hours practising in the saddle with lance and mace, his skills being tested in tournaments, if not actually in battle.

But things had moved on a bit since the Anglo-Saxon age. Knights were also supposed to be superbly well-equipped in a range of softer, more sociable accomplishments. The word 'gentle' itself was cognate with 'genteel' and 'gentility'; just as 'courtesy' came directly from the 'court' – that little social circle clustering around a king or leading lord. By the same token, 'chivalry' (from chevalier, of course) towards women was also seen as a mark of superior breeding – both in upbringing and in ancestry.

Again, the assumption was that the knight's courage and accomplishment in arms were what enabled him to exercise mercy, compassion and politeness, his mild-manneredness a measure of his strength.

The knight was supposed to be the protector of all the weak, but of women especially. Naturally enough, this had important implications for relations between the sexes. Chivalric society wasn't just about long evenings feasting and carousing with comrades, but gentler afternoons offering chaste compliments to fine ladies. 'Courtly love', as it has come to be called, had its own exacting etiquette. Highly stylized, it seems in the sources to have been as much about pursuit through poetic praise as about consummation, Sir Lancelot's explicitly described adultery with Arthur's Queen Guinevere, in Chrétien's telling of his story, very much the exception rather than the rule.

Iamque domos patrias Scithice post aspera gentis
Prelia laurigero &c
Heere bigynneth the knyghtes tale
Whilom as olde stories tellen us
Ther was a duc that highte Theseus
Of Athenes he was lord and governour
And in his tyme swich a conquerour
That gretter was ther noon under the sonne
Ful many a riche contree hadde he wonne
What with his wysdom and his chivalrie
He conquered al the regne of Femenye
That whilom was ycleped Scithia
And wedded the queene Ypolita
And broghte hire hoom with hym in his contree
With muchel glorie and greet solempnytee
And eek hir faire suster Emelye
And thus with victorie and with melodye
Lete I this noble duc to Athenes ryde
And al his hoost in armes hym bisyde
And certes if it nere to long to heere

**LEFT: As established by the Arthurian myths, the paradigm of chivalry was set out in the description of the Knight in Chaucer's *Canterbury Tales*.**

**OPPOSITE: The courtly lover's subservience before his lady is clear in this illustration from a fourteenth-century German book. She is remote, high up above him in her tower.**

turned out to have been one of the maidens he'd saved in the course of his earlier adventures. Before Gawain could raise his arm to fight, Lancelot arrived and took on Maleagant. So full of fury was the villain to see his scheme upset that he lost his accustomed cool and cunning. Flying into a rage, he rushed in unheeding and was quickly killed.

## A strange guest

Sir Gawain was also an important figure in his own right. Especially in his part as protagonist in one of the fourteenth century's most important works of literature: the anonymous poem *Sir Gawain and the Green Knight*.

Christmas had come and gone at Camelot in 'rich revelry and reckless mirth'. The world's most handsome lords were celebrating with its 'comeliest king' and 'loveliest ladies'. Party games were played and gifts were given. A joyful Guinevere presided over the scene, framed by stunning hangings of Toulouse silk and tapestries from Turkestan.

**BELOW: The Green Knight rides over the bridge into Camelot.**

The festivities were still in full flight when dinner was readied, on New Year's Day. All were assembled, to eat and drink their fill. But King Arthur had made a rule with himself never to embark on such an important meal until he'd been told some extraordinary story of mythic adventures, exploits in war – or who knew what else.

## Rhapsody in green

His wish was to be granted in a way he could never have expected. A hush descended on the hall as a giant man strode abruptly in. A terrible figure – the biggest in the world; not just tall but massively thick-set

Grave Chůnrat vō kilchberg.

and powerful. Tall and handsome as he was, he had a certain elfin way about him. And he was bright green from head to foot.

Not just dressed in green – though he was, from the ermine-trimmed hood of his mantle to his coat and his hose – but bodily. His face, his hair, his bare feet … all were bright green. As was the giant horse he had brought with him into the hall. He wore no armour; had no shield nor sword. In one green hand he held a holly bough ('greatest in greenness when the woods are bare'); in the other a huge and monstrous axe – 'a hideous thing for anyone to have to describe in words'.

With his accustomed courtesy, Arthur invited the visitor to sit and join them, but he refused. He had come to invite them to take part in a game with him, he said. If he was looking for a challenge to a fight, the king assured him, he had come to the right place – Camelot had the boldest, most valiant knights in all the world. But the Green Knight just laughed. All he could see about him here were 'beardless children', he said. He merely wanted someone to join him in a light-hearted Christmas game.

**'BE SURE TO COME AS YOU HAVE PROMISED, GAWAIN. YOU WILL FIND ME AT THE GREEN CHAPEL, IF YOU REALLY LOOK. COME, OR BE CALLED A COWARD.'**

## A grim game

Whoever here was prepared to strike him a blow with it, the Green Knight said, could keep the great axe he carried in his hand. As long as he would pledge to seek him out and take his own blow in return, a year and a day from then.

Silence fell upon the hall. There seemed no possibility of harm here, given that the Green Knight had willingly granted his challenger the right to strike him first. Yet no one felt inclined to play his 'game'; all fell sheepishly quiet as their visitor laughed, asking rhetorically whether he could really be at Camelot, with all its famous knights. With the honour of his court at stake, King Arthur himself was on the point of accepting the challenge when Sir Gawain stepped up and said that he would take it on.

Stooping a little to lay bare his neck, the Green Knight stood to take his blow. Sir Gawain gripped the axe and swung it high. With perfect precision, he brought it crisply down and neatly beheaded his opponent. His head spun smartly to the floor amid a spurt of blood.

**ABOVE: The Green Knight makes his first appearance before an astonished, awestruck court.**

But the Green Knight stood there still – at least his legs and trunk did, apparently unconcerned. The body bent down and grabbed the head by its green hair. It mounted its horse and held its head up to face the frightened Guinevere; then the head addressed itself to Gawain in these words: 'Be sure to come as you have promised, Gawain. You will find me at the Green Chapel, if you really look. Come, or be called a coward.' He spurred his horse and trotted out, leaving the company nonplussed.

They'd had the extraordinary story Arthur had wanted – but much more than anyone had bargained for. Gawain's situation now was sobering. But he put a brave face on it – as did Arthur, for the frightened Guinevere's sake. They hung the axe high up on the wall, and the revelry resumed.

## Coming due

Soon, the festive season was over. After the long haul through the latter weeks of winter came 'crabbed Lent' – a time of solemn prayer and fasting. Then it was Easter, though, and the reawakening of the world with the coming of spring – birds sang, blossoms burst forth and the woods were clothed in green. Time moved swiftly: the summer was with them before they knew it and then the leaves began to brown and curl and fall as autumn came. Gawain delayed his departure as long as he dared, but by 1 November, All Hallows' Day, he knew it was time for him to set out to find the Green Knight to repay his debt.

For weeks he travelled northwards, skirting the mountains of North Wales and crossing the Dee to continue up through the 'wilderness of Wirral'. By mountains, valleys and cliffs he rode, fording rivers and splashing across lakes and streams. No one he asked could tell him where the Green Chapel was. On Christmas Eve, he finally came to a handsome castle. It opened wide its gates to let him in.

RIGHT: This picture, showing Gawain beheading the Green Knight, is in the original manuscript, which was written towards the end of the fourteenth century.

## A genial host

The man who welcomed him was a big, fine figure – a fit lord for such a place, Sir Gawain thought. He invited Gawain to stay and dine with him. At dinner that evening, his host introduced his beautiful young wife (more lovely even than Guinevere, Gawain thought). And another woman, much older and more wrinkled and withered – but still honoured by all.

The days went by in fun and feasting; Gawain's host was the life and soul. Eventually, though, the knight recalled his vow. With just three days to go before he had to be at the Green Chapel, he asked the lord if he could tell him where it was. It was just a couple of miles away, his host replied. He could stay with him until it was time to make his rendezvous. It was such an honour for them to have a guest from King Arthur's court.

## Another game

He proposed a game, to make his time at the castle more interesting. Every day early, he told Gawain, he went out hunting. He undertook to give his guest whatever he caught in the woods that morning – in return, Gawain should give him anything that he might gain.

Gawain agreed and went to bed. The next morning at dawn the lord's wife stole into his room. He pretended to be asleep as she approached. Pushing aside the curtain of his four-poster bed, she sat upon it and woke him flirtatiously. She tried to seduce him, but he held firm, returning nothing but politeness. One kiss he finally gave her as a courtesy.

**PUSHING ASIDE THE CURTAIN OF HIS FOUR-POSTER BED, SHE SAT UPON IT AND WOKE HIM FLIRTATIOUSLY. SHE TRIED TO SEDUCE HIM, BUT HE HELD FIRM, RETURNING NOTHING BUT POLITENESS.**

The lord returned and in the hall that night gave Gawain a deer that he'd killed in the woods that day. Gawain embraced him and kissed him chastely in return. Next morning, his host went forth again – and into this bedchamber came his lady wife. Again, Gawain rebuffed her advances as politely as he could. She reproached him for his lack of gallantry. King Arthur's knights were nothing like as chivalrous as she'd been led to believe, she protested crossly. He had to give her two kisses before she'd go. That evening, his host gave him the great boar he had killed. Gawain reached gently round his neck and kissed him twice.

## A secret sash

The third morning was New Year's Day. The lord of the castle went out into a bright and frosty dawn. In no time at all his baying hounds were on a fox's trail. It was wily and resourceful, and led the hunt a dance; the day was well-advanced by the time they had caught and killed it. But at home his lady was hunting too. Into Gawain's bedchamber she crept once more. He was hurting her feelings, she admonished him indignantly. If he didn't have a love already, why was he rejecting her?

Gawain protested that he didn't. Neither, however, did he want one. For her he had nothing but the highest respect and admiration. She was not to be placated. Even when he'd kissed her three times she insisted that he take a keepsake from her. He refused – he was travelling light, without so much as a squire to carry things for him. So she held out an exquisite jewelled ring: it was enormously valuable, she told him. He refused: he couldn't possibly accept it, he insisted.

**HIS YEAR AND A DAY WERE UP AT LAST.**

Why not?, she demanded. Was he so unwilling to be under any obligation to her? He'd take something less valuable, then, he agreed, to allay her anger. She handed him a pretty silken sash of green; he took it with reluctance – especially when she swore him not to tell her husband.

That evening when the lord returned, his guilty conscience pricking him, Gawain didn't even wait for him to hand over his day's catch, but went straight up to him, embraced him and kissed him three times. He was lucky to have had such merchandize, his host chaffed him good-humouredly; as long as he hadn't been compelled to overpay. He'd certainly done better than he himself had in his hunting. He threw down the pelt of the fox, which was all he'd caught. Gawain said nothing of the sash.

## Settling up

The next morning he had to go: his year and a day were up at last and he had to go to the Green Chapel to find the Knight. Wrapping the sash around his waist discreetly, he dressed for the road, took his leave and set off to meet his destiny. His host sent a servant with him as his guide. After a while, the man pulled up his mount. He'd go no further with Sir Gawain, he insisted.

**LEFT: The lady of the castle tests Sir Gawain's virtue while her lord is out hunting game.**

The place that they had come to was held to be 'full perilous', he said, the man who lived there reputed to be 'the worst on earth'. He begged Gawain to turn back, too, and leave him alone. He promised he would never tell anybody if he did.

Gawain thanked him for what he took to be his straight and sincere advice. But he was a knight and could not break his word. He appreciated the man's loyalty but had to go forward to face his fate. It was God's will; he would not weep nor moan.

The chapel when he found it was an 'evil' place; not much more than a cave or even just a cleft in a crag, it was dark and poky and badly overgrown. The 'cursedest kirk' the knight had ever seen. It appeared deserted. Even so, he called aloud to announce himself to whoever happened to be there. 'Wait,' came the reply. The Green Knight appeared atop the crag and clambered down, a giant Danish axe over his shoulder.

**ABOVE: Gawain kneels before King Arthur and Guinevere on his return to Camelot. Fittingly, for he has been humbled by his failings.**

## Final payment

He thanked Gawain for coming; hoped he wouldn't object to keeping his promise to him. Gawain assured him that he felt no grudge against him. Bending down, he bared his neck without demur. As the Green Knight raised the great axe, though, and its blade hissed down through the frosty air, he couldn't help flinching – so the Knight cut short his stroke. He hadn't moved when Gawain had to take his blow the year before, he reminded Gawain.

Once more he raised the axe and brought it swinging down. This time Gawain didn't flinch, but the Green Knight hadn't been sure he wouldn't, he said. Again he cut short his stroke: he'd been testing him, he said. Angry now, Gawain told him to stop threatening and strike him once and for all. The Green Knight was too scared to deliver the blow, he chided.

One last time, then, the Green Knight raised the axe and brought it swiftly down. This time it struck him – but only glancingly. One little nick on his bare neck: the blood spurted out a spear's length. But Gawain was alive. He leapt forward, turned and drew his sword. He was ready to fight now to defend himself.

## Paid in full

The Green Knight looked on and laughed; he leant on the handle of his axe and smiled in amusement. There was no need for Gawain to strike such attitudes, he said. Gawain had paid his debt to him in full. For he had dealt frankly with him, he knew. Not only had he come to find him here, but he had also been an honourable guest. As promised, he'd delivered to him the kiss his wife had given him the first day; and the two she'd given him the second.

Hence the two feints he'd made with the axe. He had no cause to kill so noble a knight. It had been almost the same with the third blow, he went on. Not quite the same: he'd nicked his neck because, though Gawain had given up all three kisses he'd received, he'd held on to his property in the shape of that silken sash.

His name, he now revealed, was Sir Bertilak de Hautdesert. The old woman Gawain had met at his castle was Merlin's sometime mistress Morgan le Fay and it was she who had given him this green form and sent him to Camelot to test Gawain's truth and the courage of the Knights of the Round Table.

Gawain was mortified; racked with shame, he tried to give the Green Knight the love-token, who told him to keep it as a souvenir. No truer man was ever known, the Green Knight said. As he turned to go home, Gawain decided that he would wear the sash from that time on as a reminder of his fallibility. When he got back to Arthur's court and told the other Knights

## Eco-warrior?

It isn't clear what relation the Green Knight is to the medieval tradition of the Green Man. This was a sculpted or painted face surrounded by winding stalks and leaves (sometimes they're actually shown growing from its mouth or eyes); it seems self-evident that this was a symbol of fertility and rebirth.

It seems almost as obvious that it was a pagan emblem, and it has been adopted as such in recent times, though it originally appeared most often in Christian religious contexts. Researcher Mike Harding estimated that Exeter Cathedral, built largely in the fourteenth century (so much the same age as *Sir Gawain and the Green Knight* was written), contained five times as many green men as it did heads of Christ.

The Green Knight of the poem is obviously at home in nature, as keeper of the Green Chapel; just as Sir Bertilak de Hautdesert is a daily huntsman in the deepest, densest woods. More than just about any other medieval work, the poem is arresting in the freshness of its natural description, vivid in its evocation of the circling seasons. While Gawain's isn't a story of fertility, it does prompt a sort of moral self-discovery and re-energized rebirth on the knight's part.

**BELOW: Exeter Cathedral has an impressive collection of Green Men.**

of the Round Table of his failure, they decided that they would wear green sashes of their own.

## Helpless love

The castle at Tintagel, on the rocky northern coast of Cornwall, is famous as the place where Arthur was conceived, but it was also the seat of the legendary King Mark. A fairly peripheral figure in the Arthurian story (he appears as a relatively distant, even hostile, cousin of the King), Mark is of much more interest as the uncle of the dashing Tristan. He sent his nephew as his emissary to Ireland to bring back his bride, the beautiful Princess Yseult. The two being similar in age and attractiveness, some sort of stirrings were perhaps inevitable – and the sea voyage back to Cornwall lasted several days.

**BELOW: We see Tristan and Yseult on the point of taking the potion in this painting by John William Waterhouse (1849–1917).**

Tristan had taken with him a love potion. The idea had been that he'd discreetly administer it to Yseult as they approached England so that, on first encountering her ageing intended, she would fall in love. But the young couple ended up accidentally drinking it together themselves one night and were directly seized by a passion they couldn't control. By the time they reached Cornwall they were ardent lovers. Yseult went through with her marriage to Mark, but it was just a show.

Her relationship with Tristan continued – now unquestionably adulterous, but justified emotionally, it was felt. Medieval morality was exacting about these things: this was where the love potion came in. It enabled readers to have their moral cake and eat it, too, absolving

LEFT: An enraged King Mark stabs Tristan in the back while he sings to Yseult in an engraving based on a miniature from a fifteenth-century manuscript.

Tristan and Yseult of culpability for their sin. It also provided an explanation for the descent of the suspicious and possessive Mark into violent tyranny in subsequent stories of this cycle.

In the Arthurian canon as a whole, Tristan and Yseult's affair came to balance that of Lancelot and Guinevere: two tales of breathless sexual passion in a courtly realm in which love was generally rather more rarefied – even a little abstract-seeming.

## Celtic connections

Nothing is known about Thomas Chestre except that, some time in the fourteenth century, he wrote a memorable verse-romance, *Sir Launfal*. This was based on an earlier 'lay' by Marie de France. Not the Marie de France who was the Countess of Champagne, though she was probably of noble birth and they were rough

**OPPOSITE: Immortalized by Wolfram von Eschenbach, the Parsifal myth was reframed for modern Germany in the operas of Richard Wagner (1813–83), which in turn inspired this painting by Ferdinand Leeke (1859–1932).**

contemporaries; this Marie is believed to have been France's first female poet.

Sir Launfal was King Arthur's steward – loved, respected and rich, till Guinevere arrived on the scene. In this version of her story, Arthur's queen and cuckolder is viewed without the usual romantic haze as a shameless wanton and capricious scold. She took an instant dislike to Launfal, unsettled by his sobriety and faith. He was ostracized from Camelot and forced to return to his Welsh home town of Caerleon. (Not much more than a village with a Roman ruin now, this town loomed large in some of the Arthurian stories: Geoffrey of Monmouth – a local boy, of course – described it as a great city; a sort of British Rome.)

Riding in the woods outside the town one day, Launfal stopped to rest under a tree. He was woken by two strangely lovely young maidens who summoned him to come and meet their mistress. They took him to a secluded glade in which stood a stunning pavilion. Inside, the most beautiful lady Launfal had ever seen reclined seductively on a jewelled couch. Her name was Tryamour; she was the Fairy Queen and she now took Launfal

**BELOW: Caerleon is barely even a ruin now but the outline of what was once a Roman amphitheatre is clear.**

ABOVE: **Parsifal approaches an oddly Byzantine-looking Castle of the Grail in an engraving after German artist Ferdinand Knab (1834–1902).**

as her lover. She plied him with rich gifts and promises to look after him as long as he kept their relationship a secret.

He was able to return to Camelot a rich man now, but he still had a powerful enemy in Guinevere, who came on to him seductively, hoping to trap him. Indignant at her advances, he told her that he had a lover who was fairer by far than she was. In a fury, she claimed he had assaulted and insulted her. He hoped, while he languished in prison, that Tryamour would come to his rescue. But she was angry that he had revealed her secret, despite his vow. Finally, she relented, but not until the day of his execution. Guinevere was struck blind in punishment.

The Arthurian legends make no secret of their Celtic origins. King Arthur first came to prominence as a fighter against the Anglo-Saxons, after all. But the importance of the supernatural dimension here – specifically the trope of the mortal man's seduction and sojourn in Fairyland – reminds us of just how strong the debt to Celtic tradition is in England. Merlin; Morgan le Fay; the Lady of the Lake … the list is endless. These are figures of English – but also of Celtic – myth.

## Sacred yearning

The rules of courtly love could make it seem stiff and stylized by modern standards, we've seen, lacking not just erotic force but even human warmth. This was one reason why the affairs of Tristan and Yseult and Lancelot and Guinevere were so important: the exceptions that proved a rather rarefied rule.

On the other hand, the sense of sublimated sexual passion created an aura of wistful longing around the Arthurian genre: poets weren't slow to see the spiritual possibilities. A knight's frustrated yearnings for an unattainable mistress; his resolve to dedicate his life to serving and making himself worthy of her: these could clearly be seen as analogous to the religious believer's yearning for his God.

**SHE WAS ANGRY THAT HE HAD REVEALED HER SECRET, DESPITE HIS VOW.**

Chrétien de Troyes had introduced this dimension to the genre early on. His romance of Percival sets its hero off in quest of the Holy Grail. It was housed, we're told, at Corbenic Castle in the keeping of the Fisher King. A mysterious figure, he was wounded in the legs or groin (so effectively infertile). His kingdom had been blighted into sterility. The picture of impotence, all the king could do was sit in a boat on the river near his castle day by day and fish. One day, someone would come to him with the right question, and he would be healed and the Holy Grail released. Until then, it remained locked up – as did the Fisher King's stricken realm.

The Fisher King's helplessness prevented his feeding his aged father. This is where the Holy Grail came in. A wide dish in Chrétien's account, it contained a single communion host that – as the old man ate it each day – was endlessly renewed.

## Percival's purpose

Percival was brought up in the forest by his widowed mother, who never told him of his father's noble birth nor his valour as a knight. As a teenager, however, he saw a group of knights pass by and was gripped with eagerness to follow them to Camelot and seek his fortune there.

On his way, he happened to pass Corbenic, saw a grail, met the Fisher King and commiserated with his plight. But he did not know of the significance of the Grail, nor the need to ask a question. By the time he heard about these things it was too late. Nevertheless, on being received at Arthur's court and accepted as a knight, and being told about the Holy Grail, Percival resolved to make his quest for it the overriding purpose of his life.

Obviously, his story dramatized a hero's desire to attain transcendence and the committed quester's consecration of himself. Just as obviously, though, it was the basis for a great adventure yarn. Or would have been, had Chrétien's narrative not broken off abruptly here. No matter. Many different authors were to continue the story in many different ways. Nor was Percival the only knight to try to find the Grail.

## Purity personified

Another approach to the Grail legend saw the Fisher King's daughter, Elaine of Corbenic, being imprisoned in a boiling bath by Morgan le Fay. Rescued by Sir Lancelot, she fell head over heels in love with him and sought to seduce him, but he was faithful to Queen Guinevere. She now invoked the help of a benign enchantress, Dame Brusen, who helped her win Sir Lancelot with a simple trick.

There was nothing supernatural about it. Elaine just plied the knight with wine to cloud his judgement and wore a ring of Guinevere's that Dame Brusen had given her. It only fooled him the one time – and he was angry the next morning to learn what

he had done. But it was enough for her to be left pregnant and (in time) to bear a son.

Young Galahad was also brought up in isolation from the court, his mother sending him to an aunt's convent to be reared. (The religious strand is strong in his background: in some versions of his story he is said to have been descended from Joseph of Arimathea on his mother's side.) Growing up, and deciding to become a knight, he made his way to Camelot but before he got there met his father along the road – neither knowing who the other was.

They fought, and Galahad bested his father, who, learning who he was, then knighted him and took him triumphantly back with him to Camelot. Galahad was soon a shining star at Arthur's court. And, despite the circumstances of his birth, the epitome of purity and chastity. It was only natural that he would be drawn to the Grail-quest.

**BELOW: The Pre-Raphaelite artist Edward Burne-Jones (1833–98) narrated the Grail story in a stunning series of tapestries. Here Galahad, Bors and Perceval attain their vision of the Holy Grail.**

OPPOSITE: **The mythos may seem limiting to us, but for Victorian artists the Arthurian legends opened up a world of expression. *Sir Galahad*, by George Frederic Watts (1817–1904), seems a study in spiritual yearning.**

## A transcendent track

In some versions of the story, he was marked out for success in the search by a sword-in-the-stone test like King Arthur's. No one else could pull it out, but he did so with ease.

Either way, he became the driving force in a collective quest that some writers say ended up involving all the other Knights of the Round Table, though others see him leading a trio, including Bors and Percival.

## Alter-Arthur?

It's hard for us to read the story of Galahad's drawing the sword from the stone without seeing it as showing Arthur being supplanted by a second, perhaps purer version of himself. That isn't necessarily what the original writers intended us to feel – the story of Arthur doing this does not appear in every version of what we've seen is a complex web of often-inconsistent storylines. Certainly, though, the departure of Galahad with the flower of the Knights of the Round Table renders King Arthur and his court redundant to some extent.

Galahad is something of a Christ-figure, not just fighting monsters and freeing damsels but miraculously driving out demons and healing the sick. And his quest becomes ever more spiritual in tone. At last attaining his goal at Corbenic Castle, he meets his ancestor Joseph of Arimathea in vision and ascends with him to heaven.

Arthurian myth, we've seen, was a big and baggy category, encompassing everything from action-packed adventure yarns to solemn spiritual allegories. At its more sophisticated, literary end, however, it always leaned towards a certain melancholy, whether this was romantic (unattainable love) or religious (the yearning for transcendence). Plus, of course, it conjured up a golden age of chivalry and honour and – let's face it – golden ages are always in the past.

## Camelot under capitalism

Arthurian romances already involved the high-medieval reinvention of an early-medieval (if he ever actually existed) king. An element of nostalgia was pretty much 'built in'. And so these stories lent themselves especially well to nineteenth-century storytellers, poets and artists seeking some escape from the grimmer realities of the modern world.

The Industrial Revolution brought Victorian England incalculable benefits – but it brought an array of negative consequences, too. People poured off the land and surged into the cities to live in poverty and squalor. Blue skies smoked over and bright rivers ran with filth. Less tangibly, but in some ways more unsettlingly, a modern mentality seemed to be reducing thinking, feeling men and women to statistics.

Economics reigned supreme, though Thomas Carlyle (1795–1881) was notoriously to call it 'the dismal science'. Radicals hated the new 'wage-slavery' industrialism had brought. But conservatives were no better pleased: a centuries-old social order based on rank and deference was – with alarming speed – being swept away.

So too were the spiritual certainties that had seen people through so many centuries. It was hard not to hanker after the quiet orthodoxy of religious thought in the Middle Ages, now remembered as the so-called Age of Faith.

## Arthurian atmospherics

The Pre-Raphaelite Brotherhood took their name from the fifteenth-century Italian art they based their style on, but Dante Gabriel Rossetti (1828–82), William Holman Hunt (1827–1910) and John Everett Millais (1829–96) found inspiration in the beautiful stories and romantic settings of Arthurian legend.

Poet, painter and craft-designer William Morris (1834–96) was a Marxist but he found an inspiration of his own in the Arthurian dream. Like the Pre-Raphaelites, he responded to the vivid stories and haunting symbolism of these old myths. In his eagerness to create home furnishings and textiles that would bring artistic beauty into the lives of ordinary people, he was always on the lookout for imagery that would speak immediately and clearly to the viewer.

His fascination went further, though. Camelot had clearly been no communist utopia, but Arthur's elite had been real and human. Their stories were reminders of a simpler time before industrialism had made faceless capitalists the masters of the world and reduced the labouring poor to economic units.

**OPPOSITE: The Lady of Shalott floats defiantly downstream to her death in John William Waterhouse's 1888 treatment of Tennyson's famous poem.**

## A dying fall

Alfred Lord Tennyson (1809–92) could hardly have been more different from Morris in his outlook, but he matched him in his love of Arthurian myth.

He regretted the growing godlessness of his age; the sense that things were changing – without good reason and invariably for the worse; his feeling that the young and brash and crass were inheriting the earth. His mild conservatism helped to push him into nostalgia for the medieval past much as Morris' radicalism had him.

But such perceptions only heightened a more personal melancholy, deepened by the deaths of friends and loved ones. Based on a thirteenth-century Italian poem, *The Lady of Shalott* (1832) extravagantly romanticizes what is basically its subject's suicide. His *Idylls of the King* (1859–85) is unabashedly sad in its reflections on what it sees as the (inevitable) failure of Arthur's attempt to build a better world.

# NOBLE KNIGHTS & LADIES FAIR

The Arthurian stories were only the most famous of a wider range of chivalric romance. England's identity was forged in deeds of derring-do.

**OPPOSITE: Lady Godiva prepares to ride, as depicted by nineteenth-century artist Marshall Claxton (1811–81).**

*May all be happy*
*Who hear my song*
*A song I'll sing*
*of Murry the King.*
*He was king in the west*
*Long as his life did last.*
*Godhild was his queen;*
*No fairer woman was ever seen.*
*He had a son named Horn*
*No fairer man was ever born …*

The romance of King Horn lurches along a little naively in its anonymous author's Middle English verse. Its lack of sophistication gives it an unwritten and so vaguely mythic feel. Beyond the fact that it is believed to have been written in 1250 (give or take a quarter of a century or so), not too much is known about this work.

Except that it seems to have typified the tastes of the later Middle Ages in its rumbustious blend of romance and adventure. And its enthusiasm for the subject of the exiled nobleman, coming back to claim what's his ...

## Set adrift

Horn, the poet tells us, lived in the land of Suddene: an unknown country; scholars have suggested locations everywhere from Sussex to the Isle of Man; from Cornwall to south Devon – even southern Denmark. One thing that the poem does make quite clear is that it was situated 'by the sea's side'. It was there that, one afternoon when Murry was riding out for relaxation with two of his retainers, as was his custom, he saw a flotilla of 15 ships approach the shore. Suddene was being invaded by 'Saracens'.

**ALL THAT DAY AND ALL THAT NIGHT THEY DRIFTED.**

That term was used in medieval Europe for the Muslim enemy occupying much of Iberia and the Holy Land the Christians claimed in the Middle East. We can't be sure, but it's generally thought that the raiders here represent a memory of the Vikings: the poet called them Saracens because they were alien pagans in his book.

His father and his men tried to resist the invaders, but – overwhelmingly outnumbered – were quickly killed. Godhild fled for the wilderness and hid herself away in a cave beneath a crag. Horn was captured, along with Athulf and Fikenhild, his closest friends. But the Emir in charge took pity on them, seeing how young and fair they were. On the other hand, he couldn't take the risk that they grow up strong and in a position to slay the Saracens, so he sent them out to sea in an open boat.

All that day and all that night they drifted. Then they were washed up in Westernesse – another country – before whose king, Almair, they were conducted. He took them in and had them brought up in the royal household, putting his steward, Athelbrus, in charge of their care.

LEFT: The opening of *King Horn* is preceded by a 'Prayer for Deliverance to the Virgin Mary' in this manuscript collection, the *Harley Lyrics* (c. 1340).

## Young love

The years went by and Horn grew up, a young man whom everybody loved. 'But Rymenhild, the King's own daughter, loved him most'. She nearly went mad for love of him, unable to get time with him alone to talk, so she asked Athelbrus to

## Hereward the Wake

This Anglo-Saxon nobleman is said to have lived in the Isle of Ely, though he's believed to have been born in Lincolnshire some time in the 1030s. A teenage rebel, he was first thrown out of his father's house for disobedience, then outlawed, the story goes, forced to live on the run in Cornwall, Ireland and even Flanders.

A directionless drifter, it would appear. But there was always more to Hereward than that. The epithet 'the Wake' means 'awake', 'alert', and it appears to fit. He found a patriotic purpose with the arrival of William the Conqueror, against whose rule he led a local uprising in Ely and the Fens.

The verse biography, *De Gestis Herewardi Saxonis* ('The Exploits of Hereward the Saxon', c. 1110), embroiders incidents of his life of adventure, love, betrayal and repeated exiles with details that appear to anticipate the action of King Horn.

carry messages on her behalf. He tried to avoid the task, but she insisted. She wooed Horn persistently; begged him to be her husband. He demurred – he was her father's thrall, essentially a serf. She wouldn't be dissuaded, though, and soon she and Horn were secretly betrothed.

She gave him a ring to wear in token of their bond and asked Athelbrus to recommend to his lord, her father, that Horn should be knighted. Almair very readily agreed:

*Horn he dubbed a knight*
*With sword and spurs bright.*
*He set him on a white steed:*
*There was no other knight like him.*

Horn repaid his master's trust, going off to war against the Saracens, who were attacking Westernesse. Smiting right and left, he sent pagan heads flying, pressing ever forward. In the thick of the fight he looked down at his hand and saw Rymenhild's ring glinting on his finger; it inspired him to battle ever harder. He killed the Saracen leader and took his head back for his king.

### Beloved – and betrayed

The next morning, King Almair rode out hunting – by the banks of the River Mersey, the poet reports. Rymenhild seized her chance to see her sweetheart. They lay together in her chamber – but Fikenhild found out. He envied his old friend now, and did what he could to destroy him. When Almair returned, he told him that not only was Horn sleeping with his daughter but that he was plotting to bring him down and take his throne.

Almair stormed into his daughter's room and found her in Horn's arms. 'Out!', he yelled. 'Leave my kingdom or be killed!'

Horn left, taking loyal Athulf with him. If he wasn't back at the end of seven years, he said, Rymenhild should feel free to find herself another husband.

## An Irish exile

He and Athulf sailed to Ireland and enlisted in the service of King Thurston. Horn told the two royal princes, Harild and Berild, that his name was Cuthbert and Athulf's Alrid. The young men became fast friends.

And comrades-at-arms, because in no time the Saracens were attacking Ireland, too. Battle was joined, and Horn found himself facing the very warrior who'd killed his father all those years ago on the Suddene shore.

*Against him he drew his sword.*
*He looked down at his ring*
*And thought of Rymenhild*
*He smote him through the heart*
*That badly began to smart.*
*The pagans who had been so fierce,*
*Now turned and ran …*

Tragically, though, while a splendid victory was won against the Saracens, both King Thurston's sons were killed before his eyes. In his grief, he asked Horn to be his heir and rule in Ireland after him, and in the meantime to wed his beloved daughter, Reynild.

Horn would not commit immediately: he asked King Thurston to hold his offer open for seven years. If Horn asked him for Reynild then, he should not refuse. Thurston agreed to this arrangement; they put the question to one side, and the years went by.

**BELOW: Walter Crane (1845–1915) produced this beautiful engraving to illustrate Edmund Spenser's epic poem of chivalry, *The Faerie Queene* (1590).**

**ABOVE: Hereward the Wake leads the resistance to the Norman invaders in the Fens. His life had intriguing parallels with that of the romance-hero King Horn.**

## Out of time

As the end of the seven years approached, Rymenhild was growing desperate. Almair had lined up a marriage for her with King Modi of Reynes, an enemy of Horn's. Though she wrote her fiançé many letters, most went astray, but eventually one got through. He wrote back to ask her to wait: he would be with her soon. The messenger bearing it was drowned when his ship went down in a storm, however, so it didn't reach Rymenhild.

Explaining to Thurston who he really was, Horn won his support in getting his true bride back. Reynild should wed Athulf instead, he urged. Gathering a group of Irish knights about him, Horn set sail for Westernesse – but when he got there he met an elderly pilgrim who told him that the wedding ceremony for Rymenhild and Modi had just taken place.

Changing clothes with the old man, and darkening his skin, he made his way into Modi's castle in his disguise. Amid the celebrations, he took Rymenhild to one side and managed to have a private conversation with her in her chamber. Placing his ring in a cup of wine, he bade her drink it. She was amazed at what she found when the drink was drained. Still not recognizing Horn, she asked the apparently old man what he could tell her of her beloved. To test her, he told her that he'd pined away and died for love of her.

## Back together

Beside herself with grief, she ran to her bed where she had a dagger hidden. She was going to kill her hateful husband and herself, she said. At this point, Horn wiped away the staining from his skin and told her who he really was. She fell into his arms enraptured, but Horn was quick to disengage himself from her embrace and leave. He had to join Athulf and the others outside the town. Reunited, they marched on Modi's castle, broke up the feast and killed the guests. The traitor Fikenhild was thrown into prison.

The next night, Horn and Rymenhild were married. A blissful life seemed to beckon, but Horn had to think of the future of Suddene. Finally revealing to Almair who he was, he took a party of troops to liberate his own country from the conquering Saracens. On his arrival, the people of Suddene rose up en masse and, under his leadership, the pagans were quickly overcome and Horn placed on the throne.

By the time he was ready to return to Westernesse, however, things had spiralled well out of control. Fikenhild, released from prison to become King Almair's trusted adviser, had told him that Horn was dead, and that accordingly he should now marry Rymenhild. She was placed in a tower, pending their planned nuptials – but fortunately her plight was revealed to Horn in a dream one night. He called up Athulf and his knights and they sailed back to set her free.

## 'England and St George … !'

St George (c. 303), the purists like to tell us, had nothing whatever to do with England. He never came to the country; barely heard of it, it seems likely. And fair enough – although little is known of him, it does appear reasonably certain that he was a Roman soldier and that he came from Cappadocia, in modern Turkey.

The story of his slaying the dragon doesn't seem to have emerged until the eleventh century – more than half a millennium after George's death. It was told in many different versions across the Christian world. A people persecuted by a cruel dragon were forced to offer up human sacrifices, it was said: eventually it was the turn of the king's daughter to be handed over. St George arrived on the scene just then. He slew the dragon and freed the poor princess. In some tellings they then married and had English children.

## The quest for recognition

In his day, Guy of Warwick was as important as King Arthur. Having made his debut in the Anglo-Norman verse-romance *Gui de Warewic* (c. 1200), he featured in popular ballads as late as the seventeenth century. In some accounts he was one of the children of St George, by the Princess of England.

Either way, he was the ultimate English hero. Well-born, without being noble, he had to fight his way to respectability; having won the love of the fair Felice, an aristocratic beauty, he had to earn the right to have her as his wife. A series of adventures took him the length and breadth of England, slaying dragons and fighting giants and other assorted monsters. He was finally knighted, and married Felice, but tormented by his sins resolved to make a pilgrimage to the Holy Land. He appears to have lived as a pious hermit on his return.

One of the things that makes Guy's situation so striking is the struggle he faces to find recognition of his worth. A chivalric hero he may be, but by comparison with the courtiers of Camelot he's a middle-class boy made good; his knightly prestige a triumph of meritocracy.

**NATIVE NOBILITY CANNOT JUST BE ASSUMED.**

## Fighting back

Does this sort of aspirational impulse help explain the trope of the dispossessed noble who, in so many late-medieval and early-modern English myths, has to fight with might and main for what is rightly his? On the face of it, such stories are frankly reactionary – accepting implicitly that individual worth is defined by birth. But they also set a norm by which native nobility cannot just be assumed; it must be won the hard way, with grit and courage.

It is at the same time obviously strong as a narrative mechanism – the hero's sense of injustice a powerful driver for dramatic action. Certainly there is no shortage of such stories. One real-life example was Fulk Fitz Warin (c. 1180–1250), the son of what had until then been a powerful family in the Welsh Marches whose lands had been confiscated by King John (1166–1216; r. 1199–1216) and given to a favoured client.

FitzWarin led a band of outlaws, fighting to win back Whittington Castle in northwestern Shropshire. He eventually succeeded – though, in what was at this time a chronically volatile region, he was to lose some of his lands again in ongoing negotiations between the English Crown and Wales' Prince Llywelyn the Great (c. 1173–1240; r. 1195–1240).

**OPPOSITE: The story of St George and the Dragon was the property of all Christendom, as this Italian representation, by Il Sodoma (Giovanni Antonio Bazzi, 1477–1549) makes clear.**

## NAKED COURAGE

A recurrent theme in the English myths of late-medieval and early-modern times was the oppression of the people by the imposition of excessive taxes. The first boroughs were becoming established, home to a new middle class of craft-workers and traders: they were allowed a measure of autonomy but had to pay for the privilege in taxes to the Crown and to their local lords.

Hence the legendary heroism of Lady Godiva (c. 1070). She is known to have existed and been the wife of the Anglo-Saxon Earl Leofric of Mercia (c. 1057), but this famous story doesn't seem to have been told before the thirteenth century. Her husband was bleeding dry the city of Coventry, its people claimed. So moved was she by her plight that she staged a protest, riding naked on horseback through the centre of the town, her modesty shielded only by her mane of golden hair.

Moved by her gesture, the citizens shunned the streets and stayed well way from their windows, so no one could compromise her modesty. In a later embellishment, one man – Thomas the Tailor – refused to respect this general agreement and was struck blind by divine force.

**Lady Godiva was a gift to artists like John Collier (1850–1934).**

### The youngest son

Another example, purely fictional but powerfully influential, was Gamelyn, whose story dated to the fourteenth century. It was later to form a sub-plot in Shakespeare's pastoral comedy, *As You Like It* (1599), though the playwright got it from a prose narrative by Thomas Lodge (c. 1558–1625).

Sir Johan of Boundys, in the poem, was a loving father who, growing old and sick, left his land to be divided among this three sons. The (unnamed) oldest was to have five fields; the second, Sir Ote, to have another five, and the youngest – Gamelyn – whatever remained. Gamelyn grew up working for his oldest brother, living in his home and labouring on his land, a sort of outdoor Cinderella, while his own fields were allowed to go to rack and ruin.

Eventually he tired of this and tried to stand up to his eldest brother. They quarrelled and fought, and, though outnumbered by his brother and his men, Gamelyn won. His brother became more conciliatory and said he'd give Gamelyn his land. All went well until Gamelyn challenged the champion wrestler at a nearby fair. He won, and

ABOVE: **Rosalind, Celia and Touchstone sit in a woodland clearing in a scene from Shakespeare's *As You Like It*, which draws on the fourteenth-century story of Gamelyn.**

brought back his prize – and a crowd of celebratory spectators to his brother's house.

His brother was quietly furious, for he'd hoped that Gamelyn would lose his contest and be killed. Instead it was the porter he set to bar his door to Gamelyn and his guests who was killed in the resulting brawl. They broke in to the house and feasted for several days, after which – again – Gamelyn's brother tried a more conciliatory approach.

He forgave him, he said, but he needed at least to go through the motions of seeing justice done. So he asked Gamelyn to submit to being put in chains until a council of churchmen could convene the next weekend. Adam, his father's trusty old servant, warned Gamelyn that his wicked brother was scheming to do him down. He agreed to leave Gamelyn's chains discreetly unlocked, in case the council's judgement went against him and he needed to flee.

His brother having persuaded them that Gamelyn was dangerously insane, the churchmen gave the order for him to be

But natheles I ne recche nought a bene.
Though I come after hym with awbake.
I speke in prose & lete hym rymes make.
And with that worde he with a sobre chere.
Be gan his tale as ye schull after here.

Here endith the prolog and begynneth the Tale.

O hateful harme condicion of poverte.
With thrust with colde honger so confoundid.
To asken helpe the schameth in thi herte.
yf thou nought aske wt nede art thou so woundid.
That verray nede unwrappeth alle þi woundis smerte.
Maugre thi heed thou most for indigence.
Or stele or begge or borow thi dispence.
Thou blamest crist & seist full bitterly.
He mys depteth richesse temporall.
Thi neighbour thou witest synfully.
And seist thou hast to litell & he hath all.
Parfay seist thou som tyme he rikene schall.
Whan that his taile schall brenne in the glede.
ffor he nought helpeth needfull in here nede.
Herken what is the menyng of the wise.
Bet is to dyen than haue indigence.
Thi self neighbor woll the dispise.
yf thou be pore fare well thi reuerence.
yet of the wise men take this sentence.
All the dayes of pore men ben wikke.
Be waar therfore or thou come in that prikke.
If thou be pore thi brother hateth the.
And alle thi frendis fleen fro the allas.
O noble prudent folke as in this caas.
O riche marchauntis full of wele ye be.
your baggis beth not fulfillyd with ambes aas.
But with sys synke that renneth for your chaunce.
At cristes masse mery mow ye daunce.
ye seken londe & see for your wynnyngis.
As wise folke that knowen all the staat.
Of regnes ye ben fadirs of tithyngis.
And tales bothen of pees & debaat.
I was right now of tales desolat.
Neer that a marchaunt goon is many a yere.
Me taught a tale whiche as ye schull here.
In Surry whilom dwellid a companye.
Of chapmen riche & therto sad & trewe.
That wide where senten here spicerye.
Clothes of golde & Satyn riche of hewe.
Here chaffare was so thrifti & so newe.
That every wight hath deynte to chaffare.

imprisoned. His brother's men came to get him, but Gamelyn burst his bonds. Adam was ready with a couple of stout quarterstaffs. They laid about them to great effect, and soon had Gamelyn's brother locked up in his own fetters.

## Gamelyn in the Greenwood

Now the sheriff's men arrived from the nearby town and Gamelyn and Adam had to defend themselves all over again. They fought hard but soon had to cut and run. Escaping through nearby woods, they met a group of outlaws who had been living there. The brigands stopped them and asked what their business was. 'He must needs walk in field who may not in town,' said Gamelyn frankly. The outlaws agreed, and willingly gave them the best of food and drink. They stayed for several weeks with these 'mery men'.

Gamelyn recognized readily enough that this was no solution for the longer term. For the sake of his peasants, he had to submit to a legal process and hope to be reinstated in his lordship. With some misgivings, then, he agreed that he'd stand trial. His older brother, at last recovering from the beating Gamelyn had left him with, was determined to suborn the jury and bribe the officials so Gamelyn would hang.

On presenting himself at court, Gamelyn was arrested and imprisoned. But now his more benevolent second brother, Sir Ote, intervened on his behalf. Presenting himself in court, he offered to stand surety for Gamelyn, leaving the judge no legal alternative to letting Gamelyn out on bail.

## Justice on trial

When trial-day came, Sir Ote was actually arrested himself and led to the court in chains. Their wicked brother wouldn't rest until he too had been hanged. But Gamelyn, Adam and the outlaws turned up for the trial, too. They took over the courthouse and pushed the judge out of his seat. Gamelyn sat in judgement on the whole corrupt legal system.

They sentenced judge and sheriff – and, of course, Gamelyn's oldest brother – to execution. Hearing what had happened, the king pardoned both Gamelyn and Sir Ote. Right had prevailed and all lived happily ever after.

**OPPOSITE: A version of the Gamelyn story appears in 'The Man of Law's Tale', in Chaucer's *Canterbury Tales*, of which we see a fifteenth-century manuscript edition here.**

# ROBIN HOOD

The legend of Robin Hood set out a special kind of English idyll: a life of leisure, freedom and social solidarity.

'I cannot say my Pater Noster as perfectly as the priest does,' says a character in *Piers Plowman*, by William Langland (c. 1332–c. 1386), 'But I know my rhymes of Robin Hood … '. The reference is important because it is the first we know of England's most famous mythic outlaw. But it's interesting too that it's attributed to 'Sloth'.

Allegorically, of course, Sloth is one of the Seven Deadly Sins – specifically that of laziness and negligence. In Langland's fiction Sloth – who makes his entrance 'all beslobbered' and 'with two slimy eyes' and won't stand up to talk, so idle is he – turns out, a little shockingly, to be a priest. And yet he doesn't think it odd that he can't recite the 'Our Father … ' – Christianity's most famous prayer – with the kind of confidence you'd expect from a parish priest …

**OPPOSITE: In the carefree life of the Greenwood, there's all the time in the world for romance. Robin Hood and Maid Marian are imagined here by Thomas Frank Heaphy (1813–73).**

**ROBIN'S GREAT REBELLION WAS AGAINST HARD WORK.**

He is, he acknowledges, much more comfortable in the alehouse than his church; far happier listening to dirty jokes than reading of Christ's 'pain and passion'. His apathy indicts the inertia of those supposed to be energetic in taking charge of English village life and helping England's peasants to live their best and most productive lives.

Langland's disapproval of the Robin Hood legend is palpable. Partly because it's lowest-common-denominator literature. No man of God should be concerning himself with such trashy, vulgar, worthless stuff. Spiritually and intellectually, his sights should be set much higher. He has another objection, though: Robin Hood's relaxed existence might be seen as representing the ultimate in sloth itself: his great rebellion was against hard work.

## Robbing the rich ...

That wasn't his only appeal, of course. Ironically, the character of the English outlaw was best summed up by a Scottish scholar – John Major (1467–1550). In his *History of Greater Britain* (1521), he explained that, during the reign of Richard I (1157–99; r. 1189–99) in England, there had flourished the most famous

RIGHT: The Robin Hood adventures were among the earliest forms of mass-market literature in England. This illustration (with Robin, Will Scarlet and Little John) came on a seventeenth-century ballad sheet.

LEFT: **Richard the Lionheart led his crusading force against the Muslims in the Holy Land, leaving England in the cruel care of his brother John.**

robbers Robin Hood and Little John, who lay in wait in the woods, and robbed those that were wealthy. The feats of Robin Hood are told in song all over Britain. He would allow no woman to suffer injustice, nor would he rob the poor, but rather enriched them from the plunder taken from abbots.

Major's Robin Hood is a robber but not a thug; a leader but not a bully; a criminal who's clearly better, morally, than those who enforce the law. All are admirable qualities; and all no doubt played a part in his popularity – but they're not, perhaps, the most important thing.

## ROBIN HOOD IN HISTORY

In all honesty, it's by no means sure that England's greatest folk hero had any historical reality at all. But a whole folk history did gradually accrue around him.

Modern historians have been readier than their predecessors to point to Richard the Lionheart's absence from England to join the Third Crusade (he left a few months into his reign) as a dereliction of royal duty. And to note that the punitive tax burden the ballads frequently complain of was largely imposed by Richard to pay for his adventure. It is true, though, that his project was appealingly romantic and he himself a dashing figure. True, too, that his brother John (1166–1216; r. 1199–1216) was a lot less likeable, and that in Richard's absence he seized the opportunity to mount a sort of semi-coup. Richard, who was taken prisoner by the Holy Roman Emperor on his journey home from the Holy Land, didn't get back to England until 1194.

It's at least implicitly suggested in much of the mythology that Robin Hood's seemingly rebellious exploits actually articulated the people's ultimate loyalty to their 'true' king. He was an 'outlaw' only to the unjust establishment imposed by John and his supporters – his apparent rebellion a keeping of the people's trust.

## La dolce vita

Robin Hood wasn't just the hero England's people wished to be: he had the life the English people wished they had. Their lives were just about unstinting rounds of work – often backbreaking; always mentally exhausting. Robin's could hardly have been more different. As important as his gallantry, his altruism and his cheery good humour no doubt were, the most crucial thing about him was that he was carefree.

Energetically so, perhaps: he and his men hunted deer and roamed through Sherwood Forest. They robbed the odd party of merchants or wealthy clerics as they passed through. They clashed with the Sheriff of Nottingham or the dreadful Sir Guy of Gisborne. They intervened on behalf of the oppressed. But they didn't work. They didn't answer to any landlord or master. Seven days a week, 365 days a year, they pleased themselves.

As Robin Hood said to Little John, in a ballad of the seventeenth century:

*… we'll not want gold nor silver, behold,*
*While bishops have ought in their purse.*
*We live here like squires, or lords of renown,*
*Without ere a foot of free land;*
*We feast on good cheer, with wine, ale and beer,*
*And every thing at our command.*

A poor man's dream of wealth and plenty, then; of aristocratic levels of leisure; and of 'command' in lives that for most of the rural peasantry would have been little better than slavery much of the time.

**OPPOSITE: Robin Hood and Little John fought when they met and are forever locked in combat in the Sherwood Forest Country Park at Edwinstowe, Nottinghamshire.**

**ROBIN CLIMBED CLEAR AND SUMMONED HIS COMPANIONS WITH A BLAST OF HIS HORN.**

## An antagonistic introduction

As Major remarked, Little John was to become recognized as Robin's right-hand man. The manner of their meeting was memorable. Robin was walking through the woods alone one day when suddenly he found himself confronting a colossus of a man: he stood well over 2m (7ft) tall and was stocky with it.

*They happened to meet on a long narrow bridge,*
*And neither of them would give way;*
*Quoth bold Robin Hood, and sturdily stood,*
*I'll show you some Nottingham play.*

*He drew an arrow for his bow – but the stranger scoffed. He was a coward for even thinking about shooting a man armed only with a staff. So Robin stepped back and cut a length of oak and prepared to fight with that.*

*Then to it each goes, and followed their blows,*
*As if they had been threshing of corn.*

They battled away, ducking, dodging, feinting – and hammering each other, for hour on hour. The stranger gave Robin such a crack on the crown that he drew blood, which enraged the outlaw. But so furiously did he fly at his opponent that he in his turn became enraged and went for Robin with renewed intensity.

Finally, the big man 'gave Robin a blow that laid him full low,/And tumbled him into the brook'. Scrambling to safety, Robin climbed clear and summoned his companions with a blast of his horn. Seeing their leader drenched, his merry men thought to give his vanquisher a beating and a ducking of his own. But Robin told them not to; the big man had been a valiant opponent and would be a perfect recruit for their company. His name was John Little, the giant told them. Naturally, from that time on they called him Little John.

## Friar Tuck

River-crossings loom large in Robin Hood's first meetings with his merry men. A runaway monk from Fountains Abbey in Yorkshire, where he'd had trouble accepting the authority of his overbearing abbot, Friar Tuck had set himself up in a sort of hermitage beside a ford in Sherwood Forest. Passing by one day,

**OPPOSITE: Irritated by what he sees as Robin's rudeness, Friar Tuck prepares to drop him into the stream.**

## The people's weapon

The longbow was the people's weapon. It was carried into war by members of the peasantry when they were called up for military service by their lords. Through much of the late-medieval period, practice was officially encouraged by the Crown. At times it was even mandatory.

It's easy to see why. The longbow was seen to have delivered a series of important victories in the Hundred Years' War against Valois France – notably at Crécy (1346), Poitiers (1356) and Agincourt (1415). England's knights had no doubt fought bravely in these battles, but its archers had made the difference in each case. Their victories didn't just cement the longbow's reputation for effectiveness but struck a blow for tradition, too, because it prevailed against more apparently 'modern' but fiddly and cumbersome crossbows.

The longbow was a 'self' bow, meaning there was no compounding of different materials in its manufacture and it was made from a single strip of wood. That wood was typically yew, prized for its pliability and strength; and it was strung with a cord of hemp or flax. The finished bow was just about as long as a man was tall.

Robin represented the people as a whole. Socially ambiguous, he was skilled with the sword, a weapon associated with the elite, but was handy with the plebeian quarterstaff as well. However, he was most famously associated with the longbow, performing miraculous feats of accuracy and range.

***THE STRANGER HE DREW OUT A GOOD BROAD SWORD, AND HIT ROBIN ON THE CROWN***

and seeing him cooking what he looked on as the outlaws' fish, Robin peremptorily told him to carry him across the stream.

Friar Tuck didn't like his tone. He asked Robin why he didn't carry him across the river. Rising to the challenge, Robin heaved the massive monk up on to his back. He puffed and struggled but finally set him down on the other side. Tuck owed him a trip across, so lightly he swung the outlaw up. He trotted halfway across, then dumped his cargo in the water. The arrogant stranger stank and needed a bath he said. Robin saw the funny side and thanked Friar Tuck. He asked him to come and join his band and help the poor.

The Robin Hood legend long predates the Reformation of the sixteenth century, but the worldly wealth and pompous pride of leading churchmen was already an object of criticism.

After the Reformation, though, when many of the Robin Hood ballads were actually composed, that sort of satire took on a sharper edge. Friar Tuck enjoyed a special dispensation, though: clearly at odds with his church's hierarchy, he was seen as a fat and jolly people's priest.

## Where there's a Will

Most of Robin Hood's friendships begin with fights. Theirs is a conspicuously manly, bantering camaraderie. Take his meeting with another of his merry men, Will Scarlet. The story goes that Robin, out hunting one day, saw a young gentleman shoot a deer. He stood out in the Greenwood, being dashingly dressed in eye-catching hose of scarlet silk. Robin hailed him cheerfully and invited him to join his crew, but the young man would not stop and drew his bow.

Robin suggested that, rather than simply shoot each other, they should retire to the shade of a nearby tree and fight with swords. That way they would be much more fairly matched.

*Then Robin Hood lent the stranger a blow*
*Most scar'd him out of his wit;*
*'Thou never felt blow,' the stranger he said,*
*'That shall be better quit.'*
*The stranger he drew out a good broad sword*
*And hit Robin on the crown,*
*That from every haire of bold Robin's head*
*The blood ran trickling down.*

***THAT FROM EVERY HAIRE OF BOLD ROBIN'S HEAD, THE BLOOD RAN TRICKLING DOWN.***

Honour was satisfied, Robin felt. He asked the young man who he was. Young Gamwell, he replied, wanted for killing his father's steward. He'd come to Sherwood Forest to find his cousin Robin Hood. Robin welcomed him to his company, gave him the outlaws' outfit of Lincoln green, but called him Will Scarlet in honour of his natty hose.

## Much ado

The life of Robin and his Merry Men may have been agreeable, but it wasn't of course legal. Even without the offences for which

many of them had been forced to flee their old lives, hunting the king's deer was in itself a crime. The word 'forest' in medieval law didn't necessarily denote a wooded area (though Sherwood Forest largely was): just an area reserved as a royal hunting-ground.

In many ways, though, the outlaws are seen as fulfilling the spirit of the law – if not its letter. Hence the story of Much the Miller's son. In several accounts, before joining the band he was actually a cook in the household of Robin's would-be nemesis, the Sheriff of Nottingham, so his defection was symbolically important.

In one story, Robin – refusing to eat without a guest – sent his men out to find a passing stranger. Much was one of those who met a poor knight travelling through the forest.

*All dreary was his semblance,*
*And little was his pride …*
*A sorrier man than he was one*
*Rode never in summer day.*

Sir Richard at the Lee was his name, and his lands had all been forfeit – he told Robin – because his son had killed two men in a fight. Even now he owed £400 to the Abbot of St Mary's monastery – money that he could not begin to pay.

Not only did Robin give him the sum he needed but Much brought out fine clothes and horses for him so he could travel in a style fitting to his station; Little John went along with him so that he wouldn't lack a squire. Again, the radical impulse is entirely absent. Robin Hood and his merry men were concerned only to restore the traditional balance where it appeared to be out of kilter.

## A weird wedding

The same might be said of the story of Alan a Dale, the wandering minstrel whose unhappy meanderings took him through Sherwood Forest, where he encountered Robin and his men. 'Yesterday,' he sighed,

*… I should have married a maid,*
*But she is now from me tane,*

**OPPOSITE: Robin and his Merry Men emerge cautiously from a forest edge in this illustration made in 1921.**

*And chosen to be an old knight's delight,*
*Whereby my poor heart is slain.*

Robin and his men took Alan down to the church where his intended was about to be unwillingly wedded off to her old but wealthy would-be husband. Robin went into the church, where a bishop was about to officiate. It only needed the entrance of the bride and groom.

*'This is no fit match,' quoth bold Robin Hood,*
*'That you do seem to make here;*
*For since we are come unto the church,*
*The bride she shall choose her own dear.'*
*Then Robin Hood put his horn to his mouth,*
*And blew blasts two or three;*
*When four and twenty bowmen bold*
*Came leaping over the lea ...*

**ROBIN WELCOMED THIS STRANGER TO HIS WORLD WITH HIS USUAL COURTESY. HE CHALLENGED HIM TO A FRIENDLY ARCHERY CONTEST, WHICH HE WON, OF COURSE.**

With them was Alan a Dale, to whom Robin now handed his astonished bride. But the bishop refused to comply, so Robin simply pulled off his robes and put them over Little John's head.

*'Who gives me this maid?' then said Little John;*
*Quoth Robin, 'That do I,*
*And he that doth take her from Alan a Dale*
*Full dearly he shall her buy.'*
*And thus having ended this merry wedding,*
*The bride looked as fresh as a queen,*
*And so they returned to the merry green wood,*
*Amongst the leaves so green.*

This time, the outlaws don't just commit a breach of the social order but an apparent act of sacrilege against the religious one. Again, though, while appearing to break inviolable rules of law and propriety, they're actually upholding the system as it should be.

## The (ig)nobility

In their way, we've seen, the Robin Hood legends uphold old-fashioned assumptions about rank and gentility. The myths are fulsome in their praises of both Sir Richard at the Lee and King Richard I. But they offer another image of the aristocracy, as well; not just in the off-stage machinations of King Richard's brother John but in the shameless treachery of Sir Guy of Gisbourne.

There's absolutely nothing 'noble' about him in any of the stories in which he appears. In one of the best known, he was hired by the Sheriff of Nottingham like a common contract-killer to find Robin Hood and assassinate him any way he could. He went into the Greenwood with this in mind, while the Sheriff loitered discreetly some way off.

**ABOVE: Robin kills the cruel and unscrupulous Sir Guy of Gisbourne, an affront to the institution of the chivalric knight.**

Robin and Little John saw his approach, and the latter warned Robin to be wary. Robin scorned such caution: they quarrelled, and Little John stalked off, annoyed, and was captured by the Sheriff and his men, and tied to a tree to await punishment.

Robin, meanwhile, had welcomed this stranger to his world with his usual courtesy. He challenged him to a friendly archery contest, which he won hands down, of course. He revealed who he was, at which point Sir Guy attacked him and a fight began.

Sir Guy was getting the worst of it when Robin tripped on the root of a tree and stumbled. The ungallant knight seized his moment to lunge at him with a dagger. But Robin quickly recovered his poise and ran Sir Guy of Gisbourne through with his sword. He cut off his head and hacked at its features until it was completely unrecognizable, then mounted it on his bow as a trophy to present to the waiting Sheriff.

The Sheriff, when he found him, was about to execute Little John. Robin told him that he had an old grudge against the prisoner and persuaded him to let him slit the outlaw's throat. Instead, he slashed at his bonds and freed his friend.

Together they took on the forces of law and order. They killed the Sheriff and escaped into the woods.

**BELOW: Robin Hood, Maid Marian, Friar Tuck and a couple of the Merry Men are seen in this seventeenth-century ballad-illustration.**

## A woman's touch

Robin Hood's Merry Men were later (in the course of the sixteenth century) to be joined by a merry woman, in the enchanting shape of Maid Marian. In her earliest occurrences, she was less than 'ladylike' in her frankness. Some scholars have noted her early likeness to the ancient pagan Queen of May, a spirit of the spring, of fertility and rebirth. (All these things had of course become associated with the Blessed Virgin Mary, to whom the month of May was traditionally dedicated.)

A consensus quickly arose, however, that Maid Marian was of noble birth, and at least a little more demure, even if the poets differed on the specifics of her background.

Her development in this direction paralleled the growing sophistication and acceptance of the Robin Hood story as a romance (a self-consciously literary, even courtly, entertainment), rather than the rough-and-ready folktale it had been before.

Robin Hood's comparative gentleness – and his gentility, his courteous way with ladies – is increasingly an indication of this. The tendency culminates in the outlaw's elevation, in a 1585 play by Anthony Munday (1560–1633) and 1622 ballad by Martin Parker (1656), to the status of Robert, Earl of Huntingdon. As such he has more in common with the

## Sherwood on Stage

Their sheer entertainment value and their social-satirical dimension apart, the Robin Hood stories were of symbolic interest too in their evocation of a life at one with nature. Robin could be seen as a sort of living, breathing Green Man. It made sense, then, for them to become associated with the annual May celebrations of the late-medieval period.

These are mostly remembered now as the original occasion for traditional English morris dancing. But the festivities also included (often crudely comic slapstick) plays, for which the Robin Hood stories offered ready-made subjects.

They survived the Reformation. In 1549, Bishop Hugh Latimer (c. 1487–1555) complained about what had happened when he tried to drop in at a village church one day to offer an impromptu service. He'd found the place shut up and its doors firmly bolted. 'Sir, this is a busy day for us, we cannot hear you' a parishioner had told him. 'It is Robin Hood's day.'

It was, said Latimer, 'a weeping matter' that this outlaw – 'a traitor and a thief' in his eyes – should be preferred by people to 'God's Word'. Despite such objections, the tradition continued to the very end of the sixteenth century.

And not just on village greens but in inn-yards, where companies of strolling players performed them. They were even a favourite attraction on the London stage. At the time of his death, Ben Jonson (1572–1637) was working on a pastoral drama, *The Sad Shepherd*, that featured the famous outlaw.

**OPPOSITE: Scathing as they were about injustice and corruption, the Robin Hood stories were unimpeachably conservative. Sir Richard at the Lee embodied 'true' nobility.**

dispossessed aristocrats of our last chapter than with the popular brigand he had been until now.

## Sir Richard's repayment

The story of Sir Richard at the Lee has a sequel. His fortunes transformed by his improbable encounter in the forest, he took the money Robin had given him and went off to see the abbot. Telling him he hadn't managed to raise the money yet, he asked for time. But the churchman was unyielding, so Sir Richard revealed that he did in fact have the funds, and paid him – but given his meanness he would give him no addition by way of thanks. The abbot was furious, as he'd hoped to have the knight's land and destroy his livelihood.

Sir Richard went back to his delighted wife and started to save to repay his real benefactor, Robin Hood. Before too long he'd raised the money to meet his debt. As a mark of his gratitude he also had a hundred of the finest arrows made for Robin and his friends. He set off back to Sherwood Forest to make his payment.

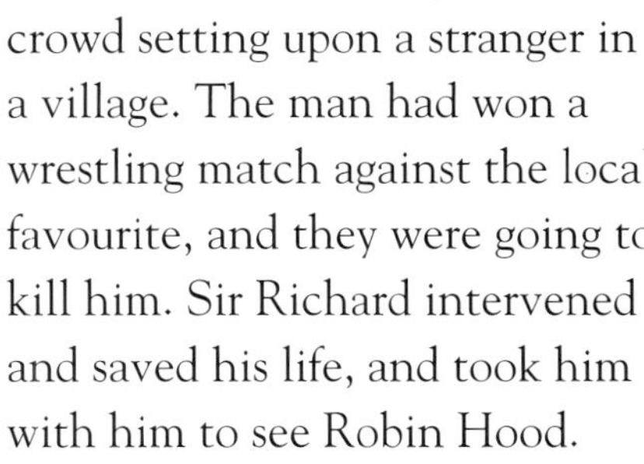

Along the way, he passed a crowd setting upon a stranger in a village. The man had won a wrestling match against the local favourite, and they were going to kill him. Sir Richard intervened and saved his life, and took him with him to see Robin Hood.

**BELOW: Robin wins the silver arrow offered as a prize at the Sheriff's archery contest.**

## A monk and his money

Delayed by this disturbance, he was late arriving at his rendezvous. Robin wanted his midday meal, but – again – didn't want to eat alone. His men brought him a monk from St Mary's whom they'd waylaid on a road through the forest. After they'd eaten, Robin asked him for a contribution – the monk said that he had only 20 coins. When his men went through his clothing, though, he turned out to have £800. Robin said he'd take it as repayment of Sir Richard's debt, since Richard hadn't been back to pay that yet. They set the disgruntled monk back on his way.

Hardly had he gone when Sir Richard arrived with the man he'd rescued. Robin was delighted to hear what he had done. Not only would he not hear of taking Sir Richard's money but he gave him half the money the monk had 'given' him by way of payment for the arrows the knight had brought.

Sir Richard had a chance to return Robin's favour a few weeks later. The Sheriff of Nottingham staged an archery contest and Robin and his friends went incognito to compete. Robin won hands down but, realizing who he must be, the Sheriff and his men tried to take him prisoner. He fled with his friends and took sanctuary in Sir Richard's castle.

The Sheriff demanded that the knight hand over the outlaws, but when Sir Richard refused, he wasn't able to compel him in his castle. While he was off getting the support of the king, Robin went hunting – only to hear from Sir Richard's lady that his friend had been arrested. Robin and his men went to rescue him, but in the confusion the Sheriff was shot and killed.

## A visit from the king

Appalled at what had happened, King Richard came to see what he could do to punish these miscreants who killed

**PREVIOUS PAGES: Home from the wars, Richard I is warmly received by Robin and his Merry Men in a scene imagined by Daniel Maclise (1806–70).**

his officials – and his deer. So as to meet Robin and his men, he disguised himself as a wealthy abbot, and made his way through Sherwood Forest with his retinue. The outlaws duly stopped him and, as was their way, invited him to dine; then to join in their customary after-dinner games.

They held an informal archery contest. Whoever missed the mark had to take a blow delivered by a fellow. Robin himself failed, and had to take a buffet from their visitor. Only after the apparent abbot had knocked him down did he reveal to Robin who he really was.

The whole company knelt to honour their beloved King Richard, who was overwhelmed alike at the warmth of their welcome and the depth of their loyalty. He was intrigued as well at the benevolence of these supposed criminals, and by the freedom of the life they led.

## Robin's blood

Just as Sir Richard at the Lee has his counterbalancing Guy of Gisbourne, so the warmth and beauty of Maid Marian has its opposite in a femme fatale. It may be more shocking to us, in our more secular age, than it would have been to the story's first fifteenth-century audience – well-accustomed to anticlerical satire – that she's a nun.

Or that this supposedly religious figure – the Prioress of Kirklees, in west Yorkshire – was secretly the lover of a local knight, Sir Roger of Doncaster. (In later versions, in which Robin is the Earl of Huntingdon, Sir Roger is a relative who is hoping to cheat him of his land.)

For reasons that aren't made clear, Robin felt the need to be bled – the common treatment for all sorts of ailments in pre-modern times. He went to seek the Prioress's help and, despite Will Scarlet's warning and offer to rustle up a bodyguard, made his way to Yorkshire with only Little John for company.

The Prioress was skilled in all the surgical arts, and set about her preparations in the customary way, but once she was bleeding her patient she didn't stop. Only belatedly did Robin, sinking fast, realize that he was weakening and dying. He called Little John for help but it was too late.

## Grave questions

An eighteenth-century addition to the story of Robin's death gave its conclusion such romantic resonance that no one wanted to do without it so it stuck. Robin, this later version says, struggled to his feet with John's assistance, took his bow and sent off a final farewell shot from the prioress's window. Where the arrow landed, he told Little John, he wanted his body buried.

And so it (supposedly) was, in the little churchyard in Kirklees. Little John is said to have been buried at Hathersage, in Derbyshire. We have of course no real way of knowing who lies where.

**BELOW: Robin's final moments are atmospherically represented here by the American illustrator N.C. Wyeth in 1917.**

## Radical Robin

Time and again, we've seen, Robin Hood as conventionally imagined ended up standing up for a relatively conservative view of how English society should be run. But this wasn't the only way in which he was seen. How could it have been, when the first thing just about anybody knew about the famous outlaw was that he had always 'robbed the rich to help the poor'?

His role in Sir Walter Scott's *Ivanhoe* revived the Robin Hood legend for a new generation in the nineteenth century. Scott may have been a conservative but he was first and foremost a cracking storyteller and men and women of all classes and political persuasions flocked to read his work. Obviously, a young tailor or factory-hand wasn't going to find quite the same message in *Ivanhoe* as an aristocratic lady in her boudoir or a well-born boy at boarding school.

**BELOW: John B. Marsh's *The Life and Adventures of Robin Hood* (1865) was just one of many popular Victorian collections retelling the outlaw's story.**

It didn't matter that, for his author, he was ultimately a defender of the status quo. For the working-class reader, Scott's Robin was something rather different: a people's hero. That he was so obviously 'noble', even though he was clearly of common birth, elevated the dignity of the masses overall. For Allan Cunningham (1784–1842), who wrote a series of articles called 'The Working Man's Robin Hood', these legends were for ordinary Englishmen and -women what the *Iliad* and *Odyssey* had been for the ancient Greeks.

More than this, though, Robin represented the real possibility of radical social change; and the power of working people to bring this about. The Chartists – who from the 1830s campaigned for a charter extending the electoral franchise to

## IVANHOE

In narrative poems like *The Lay of the Last Minstrel* (1805) and *Marmion* (1808) and novels like *Waverley* (1814) and *Rob Roy* (1817), Sir Walter Scott (1771–1832) single-handedly shaped a new identity for Scotland. It was extravagantly romantic yet at the same time cautiously conservative; stirringly patriotic yet quietly loyal to the British Union.

In 1818, he set out to do something of the same for England. In *Ivanhoe*, the rebellious role that might have been given to heroic Presbyterian Covenanters or Jacobite Highlanders in an earlier work was played by Anglo-Saxons chafing under the Norman yoke. Wilfred of Ivanhoe is torn between his duty to his father – who yearns for a restoration of Saxon rule – and his admiration for the (Norman-descended) King Richard I.

Robin of Locksley, as Scott calls Robin Hood, is an important figure in the novel. He and his Merry Men are what amounts to a militia – a sort of Saxon guerrilla force in King Richard's cause.

IVANHOE

A ROMANCE

BY SIR WALTER SCOTT, BART.

Rowena crowning Ivanhoe at the Tournament

EDINBURGH
ADAM AND CHARLES BLACK
1873.

include unpropertied men – certainly weren't slow to see the relevance of Robin Hood's activities to them. Featuring Robin in his novel *Royston Gower* (1838), the working-class poet and novelist Thomas Miller characterized him not as a robber but as a 'reformer'.

The Chartist poet William James Linton (1812–97) saw Robin more radically still as an insurgent, fighting a guerrilla action against a repressive Norman state. (It is interesting how completely Scott's suggestion of a Saxon uprising against a foreign foe seems to have been accepted at this time, scant as the historical evidence is for any such unrest.) The 'Normans' of Linton's own day were of course nominally 'English': the ruling class who lived parasitically upon the working poor.

# FROM THE PIXIES TO PUCK

A great many different spirits have flitted in and out of the English mythic tradition. Many of them can be categorized – at least loosely – as fairies.

Even today, Cornwall can seem surprisingly far away from just about anywhere else in England, though millions of holidaymakers manage to make the trip each year. For the most part, they congregate around the coast, in the county's innumerable picturesque fishing villages and surf-resorts, so the interior still has a faintly forgotten feel. A modern highway system has brought it within a few hours' drive of London and the mainline rail connection dates back a century and a half, but Cornwall has the character of a much remoter place.

**OPPOSITE: In the eerie imagination of Henry Fuseli (1741–1826), the Fairy Queen Titania dotes on a donkey-headed Bottom the Weaver in a celebrated scene from Shakespeare's *A Midsummer Night's Dream*.**

## 'Persons of a small stature'

How much more so must it have seemed when, in 1645, a young servant-girl called Ann Jeffries first fell in with her fairy friends in the village of St Teath. She was just 19, and working in the household of the Pitt family, and was apparently knitting in the garden there when she met 'six Persons of a small Stature, all clothed in green'. They 'hopped over the hedge before her', she subsequently reported.

Ann was ill for some time after this initial encounter. Her shock had left her 'so very sick that she could not … stand on her Feet'. But she recovered to find herself with healing powers. Patients came to see her from villages the length and breadth of Cornwall – and in a few cases, it was said, even from London.

Meanwhile Ann was still seeing and conversing with the fairies. More than this, she maintained, they were bringing her special enchanted bread that meant she could do without normal food – which she consequently refused. It wasn't long before her claims came to the attention of the authorities. They didn't find her story as engaging as we might now.

**SHE RECOVERED TO FIND HERSELF WITH HEALING POWERS.**

## Fairies and faith

For one thing, the old folk-beliefs that they harked back to belonged to a pre-Reformation age. It wasn't that the Catholic Church had accepted the existence of fairies. But, not seeing the possibility of any such spirit posing any threat to the Christian faith, it had regarded the belief in them with amused indulgence.

Its priests would have been bemused at the alarmist view of King James I (1566–1625; r. 1603–25; as James VI of Scotland, 1567–1625) that 'these kind of sprites that are called vulgarlie the Fayrie' were a way of 'the Devils conversing in the earth'. Even if they had been, the Catholic clergy tended to believe, they wouldn't have been any match for the Virgin Mary, the angels or the saints.

'Heretics' by the thousand could testify to the torture and abuse the Church meted out to those who differed from its strict doctrinal line. A great many weren't left in a position to bear witness, of course, because they were killed. So there's no suggestion that Catholicism was tolerant or broad-minded. But the great witch-hunts and persecutions of popular superstitions like Ann Jeffries' had, ironically, to wait for a seemingly more sensible, rational, post-Reformation age. It's no surprise to find that among the offences for which Ann was now consigned to

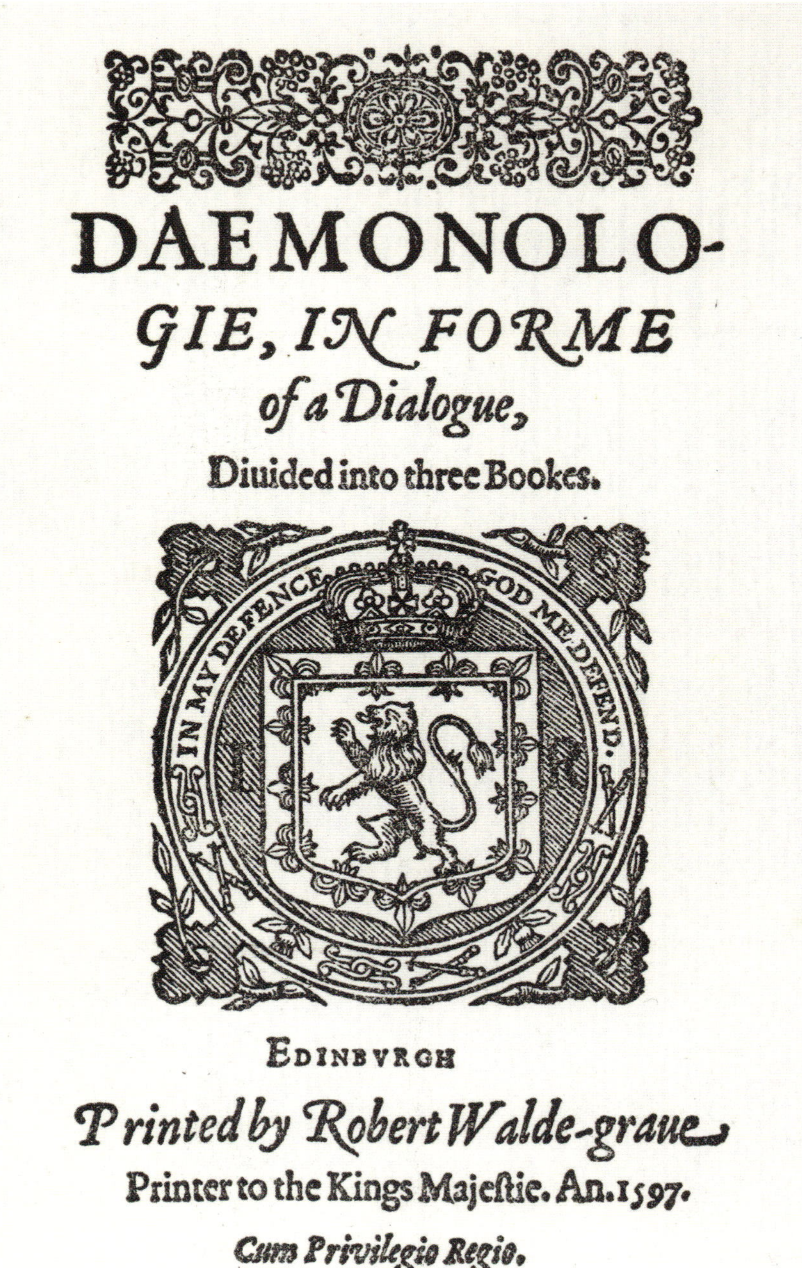

DAEMONOLO-
GIE, IN FORME
of a Dialogue,
Diuided into three Bookes.

IN MY DEFENCE GOD ME DEFEND.
I R

EDINBVRGH

Printed by Robert Walde-graue
Printer to the Kings Majeſtie. An. 1597.
Cum Privilegio Regio.

LEFT: **The standard seventeenth-century English work on the dangers represented by witchcraft was written by no less a personage than King James I.**

Bodmin Gaol was her alleged attempt to promote 'the old form of prayer'.

## Omfra and others

Cornwall has always been the most 'Celtic' part of England, the least comprehensively 'Anglo-Saxonized'. The Cornish language

**ABOVE: Sculptor Marilyn Collins created this mischievous-looking Spriggan statue, peeping out at passers-by in Crouch End, London's Parkland Walk, since 1993.**

didn't die out until towards the end of the eighteenth century. (It has recently been revived.) So it's no great surprise that fairy-belief should have had more currency there than in other places. Or that there should have been a greater variety of supernatural beings of this kind.

Pixies are small and perky – sometimes mischievous but ultimately benign. They love to laugh and sing and dance in rings. It was for just this purpose that 600 were one night said to have gathered on north Cornwall's Trevose Head. The proceedings were brought to an unceremonious halt when one of their number, Omfra, lost his laugh.

His quest to find it took him through a series of old barrows among sleeping kings, down into Dozmary Pool (a supposedly bottomless pond on Bodmin Moor) until he finally found King Arthur, who gave him his laugh back as a chough. Though rare these days, this black but red-billed bird was once a familiar sight on Cornwall's clifftops. And its cackling call can sound rather like a laugh.

Altogether more sinister was the Spriggan, which was mostly to be seen (it's said) in West Penwith, the peninsula at Cornwall's western tip, around Land's End. Where the pixie was childlike – in both stature and innocence – the Spriggan presented as squat, ugly and grotesquely old. It was associated with old things, seen around ruined houses, derelict mineworkings and farmbuildings, prehistoric barrows and stone cairns.

Spriggans were obnoxious. At its very best, their behaviour had a malicious edge. They played practical jokes – whipping up storms to harass ships and travellers overland. Or causing buildings to collapse or sending pests to spoil harvests or spread livestock diseases. Sometimes they snatched away mortal infants and left their hideous changelings in their place.

A different type of spirit, the Knocker, was said to live in Cornwall's tin mines. They were named for the noise they made as they moved about – the miners would hear strange bangs from distant tunnels as they worked. Though in their appearance they don't seem to have been all that different from the Spriggans, they were friendly spirits who looked out for the workers while they were underground. (The grateful miner would traditionally leave a corner of his lunchtime pasty behind as the Knocker's share.)

**SOMETIMES THEY SNATCHED AWAY MORTAL INFANTS.**

## Goodfellows?

It is hard to know how far this variety of spirits represents the breadth of the Cornish mythic imagination and how far it rather reflects its length in terms of historical chronology. Is the Spriggan malicious because he's a hangover of the seventeenth century's (literal) demonization of the fairy folk, for instance, while the pixies are a memory of earlier – more easy-going – times?

We do see something of the same range in the wider English heritage, though most writers make a point of deprecating and distancing themselves from supernatural beliefs of this sort – except where, like Shakespeare in *A Midsummer Night's Dream* (c. 1595), they're self-consciously exploring the realm of myth and enchantment. Puck in that play, the attendant to Oberon, the Fairy King, is a witty and mercurial domestic sprite.

**ABOVE: Shakespeare's Puck can 'put a girdle round the earth in forty minutes'. Wherever he goes, he leaves chaos and confusion in his wake.**

You would hardly call him diabolical, though the mischievous pranks he pulls to entertain his lord can certainly be cruel and spiteful. The more so for their complete gratuitousness. He will, for example, torment a stallion by 'neighing in likeness of a filly foal'. Or, he gloats, he'll 'lurk' in an old woman's drinking bowl – floating in her ale in the form of a roasted crab-apple:

*And when she drinks, against her lips I bob*
*And on her wither'd dewlap pour the ale.*

His malice has a misogynistic edge – perhaps reflecting his master's resentment of his Queen Titania. He delights, he says, in taking the form of a three-legged stool for some dignified old lady to sit on while she discourses on some matter of solemnity, then in collapsing so she topples down upon her backside while her audience roars with laughter.

He's something of a bully, in other words. It is interesting that he is also known as 'Robin Goodfellow' in Shakespeare's play. This title appears to have been endowed in a placatory spirit, rather as American gangsters have been hailed as 'goodfellas'. (You call them 'good' because you don't want them to be bad to you.)

## The fairy future

It's in this same play, though, that Shakespeare 'invents' the tiny, cute, benevolent fairies we think of nowadays. Titania, like her husband Oberon, is very much like a mortal human in both her beauties and her flaws. But her helpers are all about diminutiveness, delicacy and lightness, as their very names – Peaseblossom, Cobweb, Mustardseed and Mote (an old word for

## FANTASIES BROUGHT FORTH

Shakespeare's plays, in their playful way, did much to reconcile old-fashioned fairy lore with more modern thinking, making a space for enchantment and for fairies, but in dream. This idea is obviously at the centre of *A Midsummer Night's Dream*, but it occurs here and there in other dramas too.

In *Romeo and Juliet*, for instance, where Romeo is reluctant to go to the Capulets' ball that evening, having had an unsettling dream the night before. His friend Mercutio teases him (I, iv):

*O, then, I see Queen Mab hath been with you.*
*She is the fairies' midwife, and she comes*
*In shape no bigger than an agate-stone*
*On the fore-finger of an alderman,*
*Drawn with a team of little atomies*
*Athwart men's noses as they lie asleep;*
*Her wagon-spokes made of long spiders' legs,*
*The cover of the wings of grasshoppers,*
*The traces of the smallest spider's web,*
*The collars of the moonshine's watery beams,*
*Her whip of cricket's bone, the lash of film,*
*Her wagoner a small grey-coated gnat,*
*Not so big as a round little worm*
*Prick'd from the lazy finger of a maid;*
*Her chariot is an empty hazel-nut*
*Made by the joiner squirrel or old grub,*
*Time out o' mind the fairies' coachmakers.*
*And in this state she gallops night by night*
*Through lovers' brains, and then they dream of love;*
*O'er courtiers' knees, that dream on court'sies straight,*
*O'er lawyers' fingers, who straight dream on fees,*
*O'er ladies' lips, who straight on kisses dream,*
*Which oft the angry Mab with blisters plagues,*
*Because their breaths with sweetmeats tainted are:*

Again the imagery is whimsical and self-consciously cute, as it is for Titania's fairies in *A Midsummer Night's Dream*. But this fairy has a puckish streak as well – hence her ill-tempered treatment of those ladies whose breath offends her. All in all, though, she's a force for good. Mab is the 'midwife' who helps sleeping mortals give birth imaginatively, enabling their inchoate yearnings to find a shape and form as dreams.

a speck of dust) – make clear. Bottom, the amiable but oafish weaver, makes it clear just how tiny they are when (IV, i), craving some honey, he sends Cobweb off to get him some:

*Mounsieur Cobweb, good mounsieur, get you your weapons in your hand, and kill me a red-hipped humble-bee on the top of a thistle; and, good mounsieur, bring me the honey-bag. Do not fret yourself too much in the action, mounsieur; and, good mounsieur, have a care the honey-bag break not; I would be loath to have you overflown with a honey-bag, signior.*

OVERLEAF: **Their quarrel done, King Oberon and Queen Titania are reconciled. In the glade about them, their fairy court carouses while the mortal characters sleep, oblivious, in this painting by Noel Paton (1821–1904).**

**ABOVE: Oberon, Titania and Puck with fairies dancing are imagined here by William Blake (1757–1827).**

Through portrayals like this – and those of Shakespeare's later imitators – the sense was creeping in that fairies were a source of entertainment rather than of fear.

Puck had represented the past, and consequently loomed large – literally: he was conventionally seen as being pretty much of normal human size. Tiny by comparison, Cobweb and his crew pointed the way to a future in which fairies were too small and fragile to be threatening. We see a shift in perceptions taking place right here. There was much in life at this time to make men and women feel vulnerable (there is to this day, of course) but there was still a feeling that modernization was beginning to take the edge off ancient fears.

## Tom Thumb

It was in 1621 that Richard Johnson (1573–1659) published *Tom Thumbe, the Little, for his small stature surnamed. King Arthur's Dwarfe: whose Life and adventures contain many strange and wonderfull accidents, published for the delight of merry spenders*. It is said to have been the first fairy tale published in England, though it has also been suggested that – at least in its conception – it was factual: a true-life 'Tom Thumb' has a gravestone in Tattershall, Lincolnshire's Holy Trinity Church. (The slab, covering what does appear to be a truly tiny grave, only 40cm (16in) long, records him as having lived until he was 101.)

**SHE GAVE BIRTH TO A BOY NO BIGGER THAN THE PLOUGHMAN'S THUMB.**

## A tiny child

In the days of King Arthur, the story went, a poor ploughman and his wife were left wretched when, after years of trying, they found themselves unable to have a child. The man sent his wife to Camelot to seek the help of Merlin the Magician, who agreed to help them conceive. Three months later, she gave birth to a boy no bigger than the ploughman's thumb. Still, they were overjoyed with their new baby, whom they called Tom.

The Fairy Queen was just as delighted. She came to see the tiny boy and appointed herself his godmother. She had her fairy

BELOW: **Tom's spell as a supposed scarecrow ends badly when he is picked up and carried off by a big, black raven.**

## Tragic Tom

He may have started life like any other fictional character, but Tom Thumb swiftly transcended that status. He became a common reference-point, a figure of popular mythology. It is this that makes the king in *Tom Thumb, a Tragedy*, by Henry Fielding (1707–54), so proud to have him at his court:

*... Odzooks! My wide-extended realm*
*knows not a name so glorious as Tom Thumb.*
*Not Alexander, in his highest pride,*
*could boast of merits greater than Tom Thumb.*
*Not Caesar, Scipio, all the Flow'rs of Rome,*
*Deserv'd their triumphs better than Tom Thumb.*

Like Alexander, who had conquered much of the known world; Scipio Africanus (c. 235–183 BCE), who'd saved Rome from defeat by Carthage; and Julius Caesar, Tom was (to the king) a historic figure who'd become a legend.

Fielding's instincts were always satirical. The king's comparison of Tom with the greatest heroes of Greek and Roman history suggested what Fielding saw as his age's instinct to expect the highest praise for the most meagre of achievements.

Tragedy was traditionally the most august dramatic genre. Its protagonists, Aristotle (384–22 BCE) had argued, should be noble or, ideally, royal personages. In awarding Tom his own tragedy, Fielding mocked his age's propensity to claim classical prestige for the tiniest (literally) of figures.

seamstresses kit him out in clothes in his right size. They made him a shirt from spiderweb; a jacket of thistledown to wear over it; hose from apple-peel; and natty mouse-skin shoes. To top it all off, they made him a fetching hat out of an oak-leaf. Thus coutured, Tom Thumb was fit to face the world.

He never did grow in stature, though he became quick and confident and played happily with other boys his age. They became less happy as time went on, though, given Tom's tendency to cheat in games and to play sometimes cruel practical jokes on them. Eventually, he found himself shunned.

### The proof of the pudding

He had to stay home and help his mother. One day, helping her to make a Christmas pudding, he fell into the mix unnoticed and was boiled inside. His mother gave the finished pudding to a tinker who happened by. Tom, still trapped, was carried across country for some miles. He squeaked aloud and frightened the tinker into dropping the pudding before he could sit down and dine. Tom managed to eat his way out and make his way home.

Another day, out helping his mother with the milking, he was swallowed by a cow – who had to be given a laxative for the unfortunate Tom to be expelled at her other end. Placed in a field to scare away the birds, he was so unsuccessful he was actually snatched and carried off by a big, black raven, who finally dropped him outside the castle of a giant. The giant stooped and picked him up and gulped him down as if he were a pill, but Tom jumped around so much in the

giant's stomach that he threw him up again. He landed in the sea, where he was gobbled down by a fish as it swam by. Straight into a net, from which it was promptly landed.

**ABOVE: Tom dances on the Queen's outstretched hand, while the King holds out a signet ring for him to wear as a girdle.**

## Set before a king

It was a fine fish, fit for a king's dinner, and so it was made ready to serve up to King Arthur at Camelot. As the king's cook got busy preparing it, Tom jumped out, to everyone's astonishment. He was taken before the king, who gave him a place as a sort of mascot at his court. An instant hit with the ladies, he would stand in their palms to speak to them. One day, though, a lady sneezed on him as he slept curled up in her handkerchief, and he became quite ill. Fortunately, the physician to King Twaddell of the Pygmies was able to cure him.

He went travelling again and was captured by the giant Gargantua and held in his castle but managed to escape and make his way back to Camelot, where he astonished all with the story of his adventures.

2

ONE PENNY

# SPRING-HEELED JACK

On the tombstone, with upraised arms and rage in every feature, towered the terrific form of *Spring-Heeled Jack.* Freezer and Links stood transfixed; their ghastly burden slipped slowly to the grass, but they remained gaping, terror-struck. Vengeance had fallen!

# BOGEYMEN & BEASTS

An alarming menagerie of monsters and an eccentric assortment of strange spirits have characterized English mythology into modern times.

The story of Dr Faustus is one of Germany's most famous myths, though it's based on a historical personage: Johann Georg Faustus (c. 1480–1549). This brilliant scholar, it was said, had sold his soul to the devil and gained enormous privileges – but paid the price.

Johann Wolfgang von Goethe (1749–1832) memorably made him his model of human intellectual ambition in both its nobility and its potential pitfalls. Does it say something about the English that their Faustus found his way around Satan more adeptly than the German original had? It surely says something about them that they thought he did. And that they saw him as a subject not for tragedy but for black comedy.

Despite his name, Jack o' Kent came from further to the west, near the Welsh border in either Hereford or Monmouthshire.

**OPPOSITE: 'Spring-Heeled Jack' was said to roam the night-time streets and rooftops of London (and several other English cities). Whether he really existed or not, the terror that he spread was real.**

He's actually named for his presumed connection with the village of Kentchurch, though he may have been brought up in the surrounding countryside. We don't know when (or even whether, really) he lived, but his story was well known and widely told by the sixteenth century.

## Contractual questions

Or, rather, his stories, because tall tales had proliferated about him. They generally revolved around his dealings with the devil. A grim subject, it might be imagined, but Jack almost invariably came off best in his brushes with Beelzebub. *The Gentleman's Magazine* (June 1801) was to sum his story up:

Like Dr Faustus, he is said to have made a compact with the devil; but, more successful than the Doctor, he evaded the conditions of his covenant, and outwitted the prince of darkness, both in his life and at his death.

**HE PULLED A BONE FROM HIS POCKET AND HURLED IT.**

Briefly, it seems, the contract Jack had signed had stipulated that 'if he was buried either within the church or out of the church, he should become the property of Satan'. Wherever he lay, then, the devil had ensured his due. But Jack left instructions with his loved ones that they should inter his body beneath the actual wall of the church – neither 'within' it nor 'out of' it, in other words. 'The Devil is in the detail,' they say, but it was Satan who didn't read the small print here, allowing Jack o' Kent to make an ass of him.

'Among the specimens of his magical skill, while a farmer's boy', the writer in *The Gentleman's Magazine* reports, 'was the time when he confined a number of crows, which he was ordered to keep from the corn, in an old barn without a roof, that he might visit Grosmont Fair! "And sure enough," said the old woman who told me the anecdote, "they were there; for they made a terrible clatter, and would not fly away till Jack himself came and released them!"'

## Spanning the abyss

His most famous exploit, however, was getting the devil to build him a bridge – across the River Monnow, in the valley between Kentchurch and Grosmont. Satan had been frustrating existing efforts to construct a crossing by the community around. Everything they built by day mysteriously disintegrated overnight. So Jack convinced the devil to build the bridge for him, agreeing to the condition that Satan would own the soul of whoever crossed the completed structure first.

The devil had it up in no time, and eagerly awaited the soul of the first villager to walk across it. Ideally Jack's, of course, and indeed he did appear to be about to try it out. Instead, as he reached the threshold of the bridge, he pulled a bone from his pocket and hurled it for a nearby dog, which pelted across after it – to the watching Satan's rage.

**ABOVE: The German scholar Faust, immortalized in the play by Goethe, is represented here by Ary Sheffer (1795–1858).**

## Dark secrets

Such stories, entertaining as they are, clearly articulate anxieties – about the devil, death and judgement – that those who told them couldn't acknowledge more directly. Myths may offer interesting insights into popular consciousness, we have seen. But even more intriguing may be the glimpses they give us of the popular unconsciousness.

That isn't necessarily pretty. The free-associating utterances of the English patient on the psychoanalyst's couch were informed by deep, dark fears – and with those fears may well come deep, dark hatreds. What else are we to make of the myth of Little St Hugh of Lincoln (1246–55) – a story in which untrammelled antisemitism meets maudlin sentimentality?

The chronicler Matthew Parris (c. 1200–59) takes up the tale:

*About the time of the festival of the apostles Peter and Paul, the Jews of Lincoln stole a boy of eight years of age whose name was Hugh; and, having shut him up in a room quite out of the way, where they fed him on milk and other childish nourishment, they sent to some of their sect from each city to be present at a sacrifice to take place at Lincoln; for they had, as they stated, a boy hidden for the purpose of being crucified.*

*In accordance with the summons, a great many of them came to Lincoln, and on assembling, they at once appointed a Jew of Lincoln as judge to take the place of Pilate, by whose sentence, and with the concurrence of all, the boy was subjected to diverse tortures.*

*They beat him until blood flowed and he was quite livid, they crowned him with thorns, derided him and spat upon him. Moreover, he was pierced by each of them with a wood knife, was made to drink gall, was overwhelmed with approaches and blasphemies, and was repeatedly called Jesus the false prophet by his tormentors, who surrounded him, grinding and gnashing their teeth. After tormenting him in divers ways, they crucified him, and pierced him to the heart with a lance.*

**THEY BEAT HIM TILL BLOOD FLOWED AND HE WAS QUITE LIVID.**

*After the boy had expired, they took his body down from the cross and disembowelled it; for what reason we do not know, but it was asserted to be for the purpose of practising magical operations.*

*The boy's mother had been for some days diligently seeking after her absent son, and having been told by the neighbours that they had last seen him playing with some Jewish boys of his own age, and entering the house of one of that sect, she suddenly made her way into that house, and saw the body of the child in a well into which it had been thrown.*

We've no way of knowing whether Hugh fell into the well accidentally while playing, or was thrown there by his murderer – nor, if the latter, who that villain was. Nor, of course, did the town authorities. No matter, they lost no time in rounding up 90-odd suspects. Eighteen of 'the richer and higher order of Jews of the city of Lincoln' were arraigned and executed, their property being confiscated by the Crown.

Meanwhile, Little Hugh was laid to rest in Lincoln Cathedral, and though the Church was wary of the case (Hugh's 'sainthood' was unofficial – he was never to be canonized), pilgrims flocked to worship at his shrine.

## Petrified by piety

Also in Lincoln Cathedral is a hideous carving in the V-shaped space between the vaulting, said to be an imp sent down by Satan and turned to stone. Two imps were dispatched and duly wrought havoc the length and breadth of northern England before coming into the Cathedral and committing acts of vandalism there. They broke up pews and tables and tore books before an angel emerged from inside a hymn book and commanded the diabolical spirits to stop their spree.

One was intimidated and hung back but his fellow came out fighting, throwing stones at the advancing angel, who froze him into the sculptural form we see today. The angel gave his companion a chance to flee, which he gratefully availed himself of. Even so, on stormy nights, when the wind whirls and eddies around outside the Cathedral, some say it's that second imp, still searching for his friend.

**ABOVE: Presumably carved on a pious whim by some medieval mason, the 'Lincoln Imp' has become a legend in his own right.**

## Mythical magic?

A heart motif on a wall above a window overlooking the market square in Kings Lynn, Norfolk, supposedly marks the point at which it was struck by the heart of Margaret Read. This leapt from her body as she was burned at the stake for witchcraft in 1590. A sceptic would say that the design, with its diamond-shaped surround, gives every appearance of having been manually carved into the wall. But who would want to ruin such an appealing story?

**OPPOSITE: A warning to all good folk: whilst Anne Whittle of Pendle (right) looked every inch a witch, her daughter Anne Redferne could have been any comely wife.**

So it seems to have been with the witch-hunting fervour that seized England after the Reformation but which really took off under the aegis of James I. The conviction that witches were at work, sowing evil and spreading misfortune everywhere, was a myth in its own right, though its consequences for men and (more often) women were all too real.

At Pendle, in Lancashire, in 1612, a dozen men and women were arrested after a series of deaths – brought about, their prosecutors claimed, by malicious spells. Though one man was acquitted at that year's Lancaster assizes, the others – two men and nine women – were executed.

The authorities felt vindicated by the fact that one woman, Alison Devizes, didn't just confess her crimes under torture but freely acknowledged them – she seemed at some level, indeed, to have believed the charge was true. Again, the witchcraft myth appears to have articulated some deeper, darker fear or feeling in the popular unconsciousness that could in some cases strike a chord in the accused themselves.

**THE CONVICTION THAT WITCHES WERE AT WORK, SOWING EVIL AND SPREADING MISFORTUNE EVERYWHERE, WAS A MYTH IN ITS OWN RIGHT.**

## The devil's dog

'Black Shuck' is thought ultimately to have derived his name from the Anglo-Saxon *scucca*, which meant 'fiend', though he didn't appear in the public record until 1577, when the Bungay, Suffolk, clergyman Abraham Fleming (c. 1522–1607) wrote of this beast as a 'strange, and terrible wunder'. Shaggy-haired, he was said to be the size of a calf (in some accounts a horse) with malevolently glowing red eyes the size of saucers.

Black Shuck roamed the fields and lanes of East Anglia in the deep of the night for centuries in popular legend – his blood-curdling howl the infallible harbinger of doom and death.

## Echoes of the past

Handed down over generations, myths are by definition a legacy left by past to present. Or, to put it another way, a people's poeticized memory. It should be no surprise, then, for us to find the tradition of Beowulf's bitter enemy Grendel living on in a modern monster: the 'Grindylow' of northern Lancashire. This water-dwelling bogeyman has long sinewy arms, and is

or the elderly down into the water to their deaths. Peg Powler performs a similar function in the folklore of north Yorkshire and County Durham; Nelly Longarms is spoken of in a swathe places from Malham, Yorkshire, to Shropshire.

BELOW: **'Black Shuck' supposedly made these marks in the door of Blythburgh's Holy Trinity church with his fearsome claws when he appeared there one night in 1577.**

## Hairy Hands

If the extended arms of the Grindylow and Nellie Longarms aren't unsettling enough, what are we to make of a pair of har that don't have arms (or, indeed, any body) attached at all? T is exactly what drivers on a remot stretch of the B3212 across Dartm have to contend with – hands tha grab the steering wheel and cause them to crash. Unfortunately, the generally don't live to tell the tale

We've said that myths represen a 'memory' – and they most often do. But they also represent our eternal readiness to come up with new and exotic stories – to enterta ourselves and to make more sense a confusing world. The 'Hairy Ha myth only entered the record in 1 It could hardly have been current very much earlier given that the fi car had not been built in Britain until 1892, and driving hadn't bee remotely widespread before the 19

## Famous phantoms

The persistence of the past into th present is represented with a spec literalness by the storied spectres who haunt some of England's most historic homes. At Blickling Hall, in Norfolk, for example, the ghost of Anne Boleyn (c. 1501–36) is said to walk in the depths of night. Briefly the country's queen, as the second wife of Henry VIII (1491–1547), she was notoriously executed – allegedly for treason, though her real crime seems to have been her failure to produce the male heir her husband was frantic for.

She spent some of her childhood at Blickling – for many generations a family home of the Boleyns – so it is natural enough that she might have returned there after her death. That said, her ghost has also been said to haunt the Tower of London, where she was imprisoned and beheaded; not to mention Norfolk's Salle Church, where her ancestors were buried – and some said she was, secretly, as well. And, it seems, at another Boleyn home where she was partly reared: Hever Castle, Kent.

### The Beast of Bodmin Moor

Reports from the end of the 1970s suggested a series of sightings of a 'beast' on Bodmin Moor – a wild, open area in central Cornwall. It was a dark colour, and feline-looking – but far too big to be a house cat. Or, indeed, a home-grown animal, domestic or wild, of any known kind.

The story was taken up by the national media, prompting more reported sightings; some on Bodmin Moor but many far beyond. There were claims of livestock kills, clearly the work of a predator of significant size. It was decided by a sort of informal consensus that the 'beast' was most likely a black panther (*Panthera pardus*), though scientific research on the Moor in the ensuing weeks and months could find no trace of any creature of this kind.

## Ghostly memories

Anne's successor as Henry's wife, Jane Seymour (c. 1507–38) is said to stalk the corridors of Hampton Court Palace, near Richmond, west of London, a haunt she has to share with Henry's next-wife-but-one, Catherine Howard (c. 1523–42). Whereas Jane had died of natural causes, in the aftermath of childbirth, Catherine shared the fate of Anne Boleyn, executed for treason after trumped-up charges of adultery.

The sensational nature of these women's stories meant they were always going to linger in the popular memory in the way that, say, a distinguished clergyman or important official wasn't going to. In a way, then, their ghosts just give their memories a sort of embodiment, however wraithlike: they are walking, haunting, spine-chilling, living myths.

## A SPECTRAL SCAM

Myths may communicate important truths, we've seen; stories can be fictional and yet still 'true'. Sometimes, though, the popular mythology can lie. In 1762, London was abuzz with news of the 'Cock Lane Ghost' – apparently haunting a house in a little street off Smithfield Market.

Soon after their wedding in 1756, Elizabeth, the wife of William Kent, had died in childbirth at their home in Norfolk. He'd moved on – and moved in with her sister Fanny. Disapproving gossip having forced them to flee to London, they struggled to find accommodation even there till they met Andrew Parsons, the clerk at St Sepulchre's church. In return for a succession of loans, he overlooked the irregularity of their relationship and let them live in his Cock Lane house. Shortly after, Fanny died – it seems of smallpox. But, the relationship between him and Parsons now souring, Kent took steps to secure repayment of his loans. When he persisted, Parsons contrived with his daughter Elizabeth to stage the haunting of the house by Fanny's ghost, who communicated with her questioners by a coded system of knocking in the wall. It was by these means that she 'told' shocked witnesses that Fanny hadn't died naturally at all but had been poisoned with arsenic by her partner William Kent. On the strength of the spectre's 'evidence', Kent was sent to stand in the pillory and only narrowly avoided being sent to gaol.

Meanwhile, Parsons had realized the possibilities of promoting his ghost as a visitor attraction. Fashionable society flocked to Cock Lane to converse with Fanny's ghost. Finally, a committee of dignitaries (including the famous writer and lexicographer Samuel Johnson (1709–84)) ruled that the whole haunting had been a malicious fraud. Parsons was pilloried in his turn and then served two years in prison – but was still regarded as something of a hero by Londoners unwilling to see such an exciting and appealing myth exposed.

**Elizabeth Parson used this wood to knock the wall.**

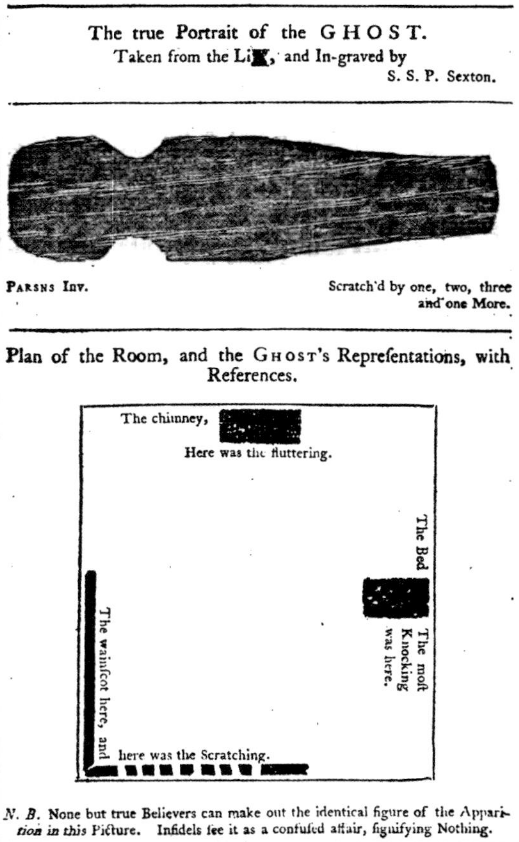

The true Portrait of the GHOST.
Taken from the Li■, and In-graved by
S. S. P. Sexton.

PARSNS INV.
Scratch'd by one, two, three and one More.

Plan of the Room, and the GHOST's Reprefentations, with References.

The chimney,
Here was the fluttering.
The Bed
The moft Knocking was here.
The wainfcot here, and
here was the Scratching.

*N. B.* None but true Believers can make out the identical figure of the Apparition in this Picture. Infidels fee it as a confufed affair, fignifying Nothing.

Ghosts may also represent important items of unfinished business – in the lives of important individuals or in their nations. So it is with Sir Francis Drake (c. 1540–96). The seagoing hero who in 1587 had 'singed the King of Spain's beard' with his raid on Cádiz had fallen from grace and from prosperity by the time he died. When he at last succumbed to dysentery off the coast of Panama it was the conclusion of a catastrophically unsuccessful campaign against Spanish outposts in the region, so it really wasn't how he'd hoped his life would end.

His burial at sea off Portobello left him with no grave in England – and hence a vacuum that was just waiting to be filled. It's surely no surprise that his ghost should be said to haunt his Devon manor house, Buckland Abbey.

Rather as Welsh rebel Owain Glyndwr (c. 1359–c. 1415) is held by tradition to pace the halls of Croft Castle, in the West Midlands – home in his lifetime to his sister and brother-in-law. Glyndwr's rebellion having ended in failure, he had eventually disappeared, and – despite speculative rumours – it was never really known where he was buried. Again, an empty space into which mythology would flow.

Sometimes, however, spectres only represent themselves – like the group of Roman soldiers seen in the cellar beneath the Treasurer's House in York. Eboracum, as the Romans called the city, had been an important centre, though the structures of those times had been more or less built over in subsequent centuries. Had these men been barracked where the medieval Treasurers' House now stood?

**STRIKINGLY FEW TRADITIONAL MYTHS ARE SET IN CITIES.**

## Natural norms

We talk today of 'urban legends'. Of course, strikingly few traditional myths are set in cities. Which is odd, on the face of it. It's true that, for many millennia, our ancestors weren't really urbanized. In those historical times through which they have actually been able to write about their lives, however, they always were – at least to some extent.

That Beowulf, Hygelac and Hrothgar live in what amount to family compounds is par for the early-Anglo-Saxon course. The story is still sketchy on its social context, by later standards. That Camelot doesn't have a city would seem strange if the Arthurian literature were telling a different kind of tale. It's an aspect of its romantic character that Arthur's court seems suspended, somehow, free of any urban surroundings.

It does, however, have a place in Nature. These romances often acknowledge and respond to the rhythms of life and growth and the cycle of the seasons. Robin Hood and his Merry Men have of course consciously rejected Nottingham and all it stands for: Sherwood Forest is at once a sanctuary, a place of escape, an alternative way of life and a setting at the very heart of the Natural world.

**OPPOSITE: 'Spring-Heeled Jack' ambushes an unwary traveller. He was unusual in being a genuine 'urban legend'.**

## Stories of the streets

In more recent centuries, however, humankind has been overwhelmingly urbanized – most certainly in England. Some sort of urban mythology was always going to emerge. Only in odd stories for the most part, though. Stories like that of Spring-Heeled Jack, a diabolical figure discussed in anxious tones by Victorian citizens of several cities (including London and Liverpool).

Standing 3m (10ft) tall, he literally had springs in his heels (modern technology taking the place of ancient magic) that enabled him to jump over terraces of houses from street to street. In many accounts he wore a big black swirling cloak; in some he had sharp steely claws on his hands and in others he breathed out blue and silver flames.

## Myth and the metropolis

The more we think about it, though, the clearer it becomes that the rhythms that really matter to us in myth are the elemental ones. Those of birth and death; of youth and age; of love and marriage; of trust and betrayal … we really don't need that much in the way of extraneous detail. The open, uncluttered imaginative arena in which mythic stories are typically set is perfectly adapted to the airing of such themes.

City life bustles with people, traffic, commerce, social interactions and sensory perceptions. So it makes sense as a setting for the nineteenth-century novel, its specificity giving an important grounding to its deeper psychological and social preoccupations. It works as well for the modernist text, in its obsessive concern with individual perception and, more widely, with twentieth-century civilization and its discontents.

ABOVE: **Through books and films and other media, Tolkien's mythic vision has inspired millions around the world.**

But it's perhaps too busy a background for a big and simple action in which broader issues of existence are in the balance; in which archetypes matter more than individual characters, and too much detail is only going to muddy the mythic waters. The attentions of modern writers may have been engaged elsewhere, but these big questions carried on being important. Some modernists did acknowledge this. Indeed, James Joyce (1882–1941) famously gave the twentieth-century urban setting a sense of mythic sweep in *Ulysses* (1922). This placed Homer's hero in Dublin, but was the exception that proved the rule.

## Of Hobbits and Orcs

After the moral cataclysm of World War I, England enjoyed a decidedly uneasy calm, as though the whole nation was suffering a form of shellshock (PTSD). An American immigrant, T.S. Eliot (1888–1965), evoked in the poetry of *The Waste Land* what he saw as the disintegration of western culture, and with it the implosion of the modern self. Meanwhile, in the spiralling rhythms of his 'Vorticist' paintings, Wyndham Lewis (1882–1957) seemed to show an artistic vision close to collapse and a society that was circling the drain.

In the peace and quiet of Oxford, though, J.R.R. Tolkien (1892–1973) was hard at work. He made himself a world authority on Anglo-Saxon literature in general – and on *Beowulf* in particular. It was from there that he took the dragon, Smaug, for *The Hobbit* – the story he started writing as an entertainment for his children but which became a bestseller (and a classic of a certain sort). It wasn't just Smaug he borrowed, of course, but his central antagonism to the story's improbable hero, Bilbo Baggins. And too many other details, influences and insights to enumerate.

## From divertissement to darkness

The success of *The Hobbit* put *Beowulf* back on the English mythic map. But it also raised tantalizing possibilities for future writing. Tolkien's reading – not just in Anglo-Saxon literature but in Old Norse stories and the Arthurian romances of slightly later times – all influenced his next novel, *The Lord of the Rings* (1954–5). This could have been no more than a knowing entertainment for his academic friends – all allusions and in-jokes. In the event, it didn't turn out that way. It seems to have taken the experience of World War II (which Tolkien sat out in his Oxford study) to focus his imagination on World War I, in which he'd fought.

Whether unconsciously or by an effort of will, he'd suppressed the horrific memories this had left him with and they are nowhere to be traced in *The Hobbit* – with all its darker moments, an upbeat book.

Somehow, it seems to have caught up with him, though. It all came out in *The Lord of the Rings* and made of a scholar's sophisticated sally a profound and powerful exploration of what it was that really mattered in human life.

**BELOW: Studious and unassuming, J.R.R. Tolkien makes an unlikely mythic hero, but he gave twentieth-century England a new mythology of its own.**

## The imagination reimagined

Suddenly, myth was mainstream. Tolkien's friend and fellow-medievalist C.S. Lewis (1898–1963) had already started building classic fiction of his own on the foundations of ancient legends. Mostly, it must be admitted, not those of the English but those of the Greek, Norse and Irish cultures.

And, of course, those of the Jews. (For so avowedly and unabashedly Christian a writer as C.S. Lewis, the Bible was inevitably an important source.) But his *The Chronicles of Narnia* (1950–6) drew out the principles that underlay all the world's mythologies, conferring order and orientation, like magnetic poles. Lewis' work was interesting too in combining mythic figures with modern, realistically described children, reconciling the realms of myth and modern fiction.

**BELOW: The English scene was reinvented as a mythic landscape by C.S. Lewis, Tolkien's friend and fellow Oxford scholar.**

Between them, Tolkien and Lewis opened the door to a new approach to writing: one that, while inescapably modern, would draw on the deepest wellsprings of ancient myth.

Their success – at home, across the English-speaking world and, before too long, in translation internationally – prompted a new approach to reading; a new appreciation of the power of myth; and a new kind of writer, creating thrilling fictions of 'sword and sorcery' and a range of other associated genres.

Their popularity remains enormous. But Tolkien, Lewis and their followers have affected our culture far more widely – in movies, comics, computer games and digital art. And, more widely if less obviously,

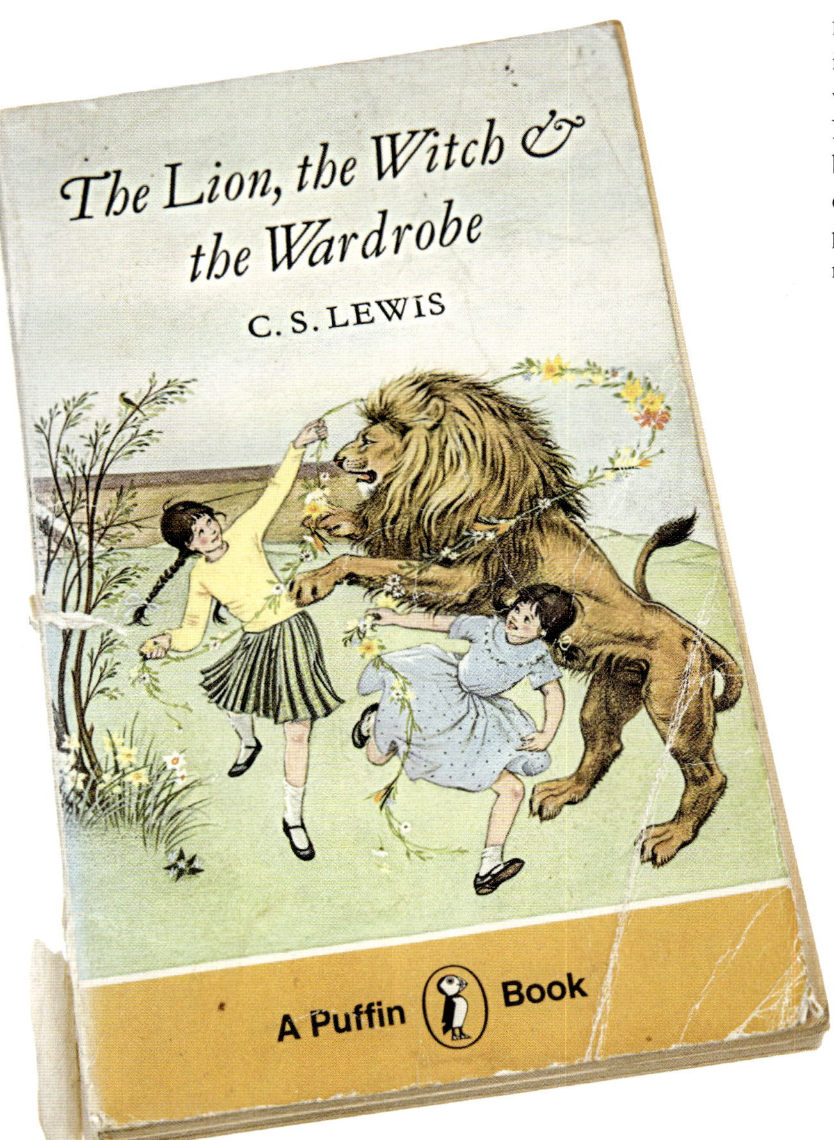


LEFT: 'I had very little idea how the story would go,' said C.S. Lewis. 'And then Aslan bounded into it.' The entire series fell into place around the mythic lion.

in opening up literary fiction, art-film and other areas of what used to be called high culture to the power and fascination of English myth.

Not too long ago this material would either have been revered (but ignored by the mass of readers) as the high-flown preserve of professional scholars or despised as the sensational stuff of 'penny dreadfuls'. Now we can see that what made these stories seem primitive makes them profound; that what made them popular (even vulgar!) makes them universal.

# INDEX

References to images are in *italics*.

# PICTURE CREDITS

Alamy: 5 (Ancient Art and Architecture), 11 (Heritage Image Partnership), 12 (Chronicle), 14 (The Natural History Museum), 20 (Martin Bache), 21 (Old Books Images), 22 both (Heritage Image Partnership), 24 (Science History Images), 26 (Prisma Archivo), 28 (Nick Harrison), 35 (GL Archive), 36 (Jason Wood), 38 (The Print Collector), 40 (Chronicle), 42 (Historical Images Archive), 43 (Ian Dagnall), 48 (Robert Morris), 54/55 (Heritage Image Partnership), 58 (Angelo Hornak), 60 (Artefact), 63 (Ian Dagnall Computing), 67 (Jean Williamson), 68 (Heritage Image Partnership), 73 (Interfoto), 74 (Chronicle), 75 (Heritage Image Partnership), 77 (Interfoto), 84 (Science History Images), 89 (Heritage Image Partnership), 90 (2ebill), 93 (2d Alan King), 94 (Stephen Dorey), 95 (Joana Kruse), 101 (PjrWindows ), 103 (Science History Images), 108 (GL Archive), 112 (Glasshouse Images), 113 (PA Images), 114 (AF Fotografie), 118 (Interfoto), 120 (incamerastock), 121 (Sunny Celeste), 124 (Chronicle), 126 (World History Archive), 127 (Lebrecht Music & Arts), 129 (Pictorial Press), 131 (Granger Historical Picture Archive), 139 (K J Bennett), 140 (Fisherman), 141 (Lebrecht Music & Arts), 144 (Sunny Celeste), 146/147 (Artokoloro), 149 (Painters), 157 (past art), 158 (Historical Images Archive), 160 (Painting), 166 (Artefact), 168 (Ancient Art and Architecture), 173 (Old Paper Studios), 176 (Chronicle), 179 (Granger Historical Picture Archive), 180 (Chronicle), 183 (World of Triss), 187 (Art Collection 3), 189 (Colin Waters), 190 (Peter Barritt), 193 (Chronicle), 194 (Paul Carstairs), 196 (Chronicle), 200 (GL Archive), 203 (World History Archive), 204 & 211 (Chronicle), 212 (geogphotos), 214 (Icom Images), 216 (Science History Images), 218 (Pictorial Press), 220 (Keystone Press), 221 (Chris Howes/Wild Places Photography)

Bridgeman Images: 8 (Biblioteque Nationale), 32 (Agnews, London), 64 (PVDE), 71, 152 & 162 (Herbert Art Gallery & Museum, Coventry, UK)

Bridgeman Images/British Library Board: 6, 34, 37, 81, 97, 138, 155, 164

Dreamstime: 27 (Psankey), 44 (Lightphoto), 78 (Sedmak), 171 (Georgesixth), 209 (Michaelbfoley)

Mary Evans Picture Library/Illustrated London News: 130, 133

Getty images: 10 (Duncan P Walker), 46 (Archive Photos), 47 (Universal Images Group), 50 (Duncan Walker), 52 (Ashmolean Museum, University of Oxford), 82 (ZU_09), 105 (Historica Graphica Collection), 111 (APIC), 116 (Heritage Images), 143 (Print Collector), 150 (Universal Images Group), 163 (Fine Art Photographic), 169 & 182 (Bettmann), 184/185 (Hulton), 188 (Universal Images Group), 198/199 (De Agostini), 201 (Universal Images Group), 207 (Heritage Images), 219 (Haywood Magee/ Picture Post)

iStockphoto: 92 (Dan Wrench)

Public Domain: 56, 134, 137

Shutterstock: 16/17 & 18 (Kevin Standage), 30 (Piranhi), 86/87 (Frank Bach), 98 (Nancy Bauer), 104 (Awe Inspiring Images), 106 (Colin Woods), 122/123 (schistra), 142 (steved_np3)